THE SUNDERED REALM
The War of Powers: Book One

FOST LONGSTRIDER, an adventurer with a thirst for knowledge and a lust for life. He befriends

MORIANA, princess of the powerful City in the Sky, locked in mortal combat with her evil sister,

SYNALON, usurper of the throne and practitioner of the Dark Arts. She conspires with

PRINCE RANN, who lost his manhood but not his quest for blood. He wants

ERIMENES, a lecherous spirit/genie who holds the key to the Amulet of Living Flame—which will bring the dead back to life!

While these mortals (and one shade) struggle for control of the magical amulet, their sorcery and swordplay arouse slumbering demons. The clash of wills and weapons leads to a shattering crescendo:

THE WAR OF POWERS

The War of Powers series by Robert E. Vardeman and Victor Milán

THE SUNDERED REALM

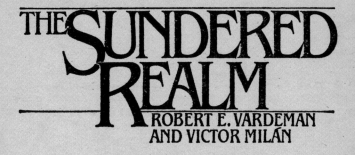

ROBERT E. VARDEMAN
AND VICTOR MILÁN

ACE FANTASY BOOKS
NEW YORK

THE SUNDERED REALM

An Ace Fantasy Book / published by arrangement with
the author

PRINTING HISTORY
Berkley edition / October 1980
Ace edition / August 1985

ISBN: 0-441-79091-7

Ace Fantasy Books are published by The Berkley Publishing Group,
200 Madison Avenue, New York, New York 10016.
PRINTED IN THE UNITED STATES OF AMERICA

For my grandmother, Frances McEvoy, with love.
—vwm—

For Hazel Slider, who listens and cares. With all my love.
—rev—

A Chronology
of the Sundered Realm

—20,000 The reptilian *Zr'gsz* settle the Southern
Continent and begin construction of the City
in the Sky.

—3,100 Istu sent by the Dark Ones to serve the
Zr'gsz as a reward for their devotion.

—2,300 Human migration begins.

—2,100 Athalau founded by migrants from the Islands of the Sun.

—1,700 Explorers from the Northern Continent
found High Medurim.

—1,000 Tension increases between the *Zr'gsz* and
the human settlers.

—31 *Zr'gsz* begin active campaign to exterminate
all humans.

—3 Martyrdom of the Five Holy Ones.

0 *The War of Powers*: Unable to wipe out
the human invaders, the *Zr'gsz* begin to use
the powers of Istu. Most of the Southern
Continent is desolated. In Athalau, Felarod
raises his Hundred and summons up the
World-Spirit. Forces unleashed by the struggle sink continents, tip the world on its axis
(bringing Athalau into the polar region),
cause a star to fall from the heavens to create

the Great Crater. The *Zr'gsz* and Istu are defeated; Istu is cast into a magical sleep and imprisoned in the Sky City's foundations. Conflict costs the life of Felarod and ninety of his Hundred. Survivors exile themselves from Athalau in horror at the destruction they've brought about.

Human Era begins.

100   Trade between humans and *Zr'gsz* grows; increasing population of humans in the Sky City. Medurim begins its conquests.

979   Ensdak Aritku proclaimed first Emperor of High Medurim.

1171   Humans seize power in the Sky City. The *Zr'gsz* are expelled. Riomar shai-Gallri crowns herself queen.

2317   Series of wars between the Empire of Medurim and the City in the Sky.

2912–17   War between the Sky City and Athalau; Athalau victorious. Wars between the City and Athalau continue on and off over the next several centuries.

5143   Julanna Etuul wrests the Beryl Throne from Malva Kryn. She abolishes worship of the Dark Ones within the Sky City, concludes peace with the Empire.

5331   Invaders from the Northern Continent seize Medurim and the Sapphire Throne; barbarian accession signals fresh outbreak of civil wars.

5332   Newly-proclaimed Emperor Churdag declares war on the City in the Sky.

5340 Chafing under the oppression of the Barbarian Empire, the southern half of the Empire revolts. Athalau and the Sky City form an alliance.

5358 Tolviroth Acerte, the City of Bankers, is founded by merchants who fled the disorder in High Medurim.

5676 Collapse of the Barbarian Dynasty. The Sky City officiates over continent-wide peace.

5700 The Golden Age of the City in the Sky begins.

6900 General decline overtakes Southern Continent. The Sky City magic and influence wane. Agriculture breaks down in south and west. Glacier nears Athalau. Tolviroth Acerte rises through trade with Jorea.

7513 Battle of River Marchant, between Quincunx Federation and High Medurim, ends Imperial domination everywhere but in the northwest corner of the continent. The Southern Continent becomes the Sundered Realm.

8614 Erimenes the Ethical born. Population of Athalau in decline.

8722 Erimenes dies at 108.

8736 Birth of Ziore.

8823 Death of Ziore.

9940 Final abandonment of Athalau to encroaching glacier.

10,091   Prince Rann Etuul born to Ekrimsin the Ill-Favored, sister to Queen Derora V.

10,093   Synalon and Moriana born to Derora. As younger twin, Moriana becomes heir apparent.

10,095   Fost Longstrider born in The Teeming, slum district of High Medurim.

10,103   Teom the Decadent ascends the Sapphire Throne. Fost's parents killed in rioting over reduction in dole to cover Imperial festivities.

10,120   Jar containing the spirit of Erimenes the Ethical discovered in brothel in The Sjedd.

Mount Omizantrim, "Throat of the Dark Ones," from whose lava the *Zr'gsz* mined the skystone for the Sky City foundations, has its worst eruption in millenia.

10,121   Fost Longstrider, now a courier of Tolviroth Acerte, is commissioned to deliver a parcel to the mage Kest-i-Mond.

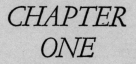

*CHAPTER
ONE*

"Up! Up you!"

Growling, the six dogs sorted themselves out of the heap in which they'd spent the night.

"We've a hard day's travel ahead."

Bleary-eyed from too much wine and too little sleep, Fost Longstrider forgot the caution a courier learns to exercise with the high-strung dogs of his sled team. He kicked out and caught the newest animal, a two-year-old named Ranar, smartly in the ribs. With a snarl of rage, the dog launched itself at Fost's throat.

Fost stepped backwards, tripped on a loose legging-strap, and sat down hard in the kennel yard. Cursing, he fumbled for his dagger. It was trapped beneath him.

The breath exploded from his body as Ranar landed atop him. He threw up his arms to ward off the beast. White fangs flashed inches from his face. Dog-breath stank in his nostrils.

Then the angry dog was no longer between Fost and the overcast morning sky. He heard a heavy thump, followed by low warning growls.

The big man hauled himself to a sitting position. His two lead dogs, Wigma and black and silver Raissa, had bowled over the offending animal and now stood above it, teeth bared.

"Good dogs," Fost called to them. "Back Wigma, Raissa. Let him up."

The dogs backed away from Ranar, still rumbling

15

deep in their throats. Ranar picked himself up, slunk to a stuccoed wall and began to lick himself.

Fost knelt briefly to pat his lead dogs. They both looked sheepish. It was their responsibility to keep order among the team and though Ranar's outburst had been a result of their master's carelessness, they felt guilty for allowing it. A courier depended on his team, particularly his lead dogs; Wigma and Raissa were two of the best.

The animals allowed themselves to be strapped into their harnesses with no further demonstration. Ranar hesitated but came when Fost called him. Fost made no further attempt to punish the dog. Wigma and Raissa had amply shown what would happen if the newcomer misbehaved again.

Fost checked the rotation of the rollers. Satisfied, he tossed a coin to a pimply-faced kennel boy who emerged from a booth by the gate and urged the dogs out of the yard and onto the road. He pushed the sled a short way to get it moving, then leaped aboard.

Southward bound toward the castle of Kest-i-Mond the Mage, Fost found sleep overtaking him. The bumping of the sled as it labored along the road hardly affected him. He'd long since developed the merchant's ability to sleep upright with his eyes open, letting the dogs shift for themselves. If anything, the rhythmic rocking of the sled brought him closer to nodding off.

Memories of Eliska drifted through his mind. *Such a lovely wench,* he thought dreamily. So passionate and comely and nakedly appreciative of what the rough-hewn courier had to offer.

The question of who had been behind the attack of the night before, in the alleyway in Samadum as he made his way to the waiting Countess Eliska ra-Marll's bedchamber, still troubled him, but he no longer suspected the lusty Eliska or her spouse. The many king-

doms and city-states of the Sundered Realm were
jealous and fiercely competitive, and their rivalry often
embroiled bystanders. Fost had probably been the victim of mistaken identity in some petty trade dispute.

He found himself eager to deliver his burden to
Kest-i-Mond and return to Eliska's embrace. Few
women could compare with the superbly endowed
countess. Her eyes, her perfumed scent, her full breasts,
her willing mouth and hot, probing tongue . . .

"I quite agree," a voice said, faint and from no
apparent direction.

Fost snapped awake. His hand moved to the small
blade sheathed at his right hip.

"Who spoke?" he demanded.

Ahead stretched the dusty, deserted road leading off
into the everlasting emptiness of the steppes. The dogs
pulled steadily, showing no sign of sensing an intruder.
Fost frowned. Many times he'd stayed alive only because
of the sensitive noses of his lead dogs.

If they scented no one, no one was there.

The terrain on either side was bleak and barren. The
rolling landscape was covered with sere, scrubby grasses
dotted occasionally with gnarled brush. Ahead and to
the right of the road, a copse of trees jostled the horizon. Even had the dogs' noses played them false, there
was no place in voice range for a stranger to hide.

Behind, the road to Samadum reached empty. The
city's outline shimmered in the heat of late-summer sun.
Above drifted idle clouds, slowly burning away in the
sunlight.

"I'm imagining things," Fost said with a shrug. The
sound of his own voice reassured him.

"A hazard of your calling, no doubt," the sourceless
voice said, more distinctly this time. "A product of too
many nights alone, I shouldn't wonder."

Fost's lips drew back from his teeth. He feared no

man or beast—nothing he could see. But to be addressed by invisible beings unnerved him.

"Who speaks?" he growled, fingers tightening on the hilt of his broadsword. "Show yourself."

"Do not be perturbed, dear boy." The voice sounded amused. "I certainly mean you no harm."

"Halt! You miserable curs, *stop!*" Fost dug his heels into the soft dirt of the road. The dogs stumbled and jerked in the harnesses at the sudden stop. They snarled and snapped at each other until Wigma and his mate restored order with authoritative growls.

"Why do we stop? Is there something intriguing to do or see?"

Raissa and Wigma were regarding their master as if they feared for his sanity, as puzzled as the unseen speaker by the abrupt halt. Fost whipped forth sword and dagger, slicing empty air.

The voice chuckled. "You're overwrought," it declared. "Perhaps because of your exertions with the delightful Eliska. A tasty lass, is she not?"

"Eliska? By the Dark Ones, what do you know of Eliska?"

"Really, Fost, I was there. Do you forget so soon?" The voice gave a very human sigh of pleasure. "Such a hot-blooded young beauty. And your own performance was truly inspired!"

Fost straightened. A curious calm came over him. He knew now what he faced.

Only one thing in the Sundered Realm and the wide world beyond would speak to him thus from empty air of his nocturnal tryst with Eliska ra-Marll. It was a demon come to issue him the Hell Call. Legend had it that only Melikar the One-Armed had ever defeated a demon giving the Call, but Fost vowed to fight well and go down to damnation as befitted a man of his calling.

Only the brave succeeded as couriers of the Sundered Realm, and he was the bravest of the couriers alive.

He steeled himself and waited for death.

"I'm ready, demon," he said. "Take me if you can."

"Demon?" The tone of the voice wavered between pique and pleasure. "No demon, I. Only the poor shade of one long dead."

Clammy fingers gripped at Fost's belly. Demons were not the only spirits a man had to fear.

"I call upon the Great Ultimate for protection," Fost said, too loudly, not really believing it would work. He'd called on the Great Ultimate before, without result. Still, a man never knew, and any ally could prove useful when dealing with the undead. "Ust the Red Bear, Gormanka, patron of couriers: I beseech your protection against the denizens of the netherworld."

"Such theatrics," scoffed the disembodied voice. "Do you truly believe in those antiquated deities? They do not exist, not a one of them. I am dead, and you can believe me. There is nothing but gray limbo, with here and there a hardier spirit clinging to the last spark of life."

Fost had quit glaring wildly at the surrounding steppe and looked intently at the clay vessel secured to the frame of his dogsled. It was the same pot that had dangled in his pouch the night before when he fought the killers in the alley—and when he had slipped unseen into the chamber of Eliska. A suspicion formed in his mind.

He sheathed his sword. With the tip of his dagger, he touched the sealed jar. Instinct kept him from doing more. A courier never poked into the contents of things he carried, especially when he served a powerful magician.

He studied the vessel for the first time since taking

possession of it. The dark red surface appeared ordinary enough, though he could make out crow-track
cuneiforms when he held the jug at the proper angle
to the sun. The lid, sealed with pitch within the neck
of the jar, was black, slate-like rock. It was a common
type of jug, of a sort often used to carry wine or other
potables.

Thoughtfully, he tapped the jug with his dagger.

"Stop that!" the voice snapped. "You've no idea the
racket that makes."

Fost jumped again. Without thinking, he cast the
jug away from him with the full strength of his arms
and upper back. The clay pot banged against a rock
thirty paces distant.

Fost wiped sweat from his forehead. He shuddered
at the thought of the breach of duty he'd just committed.
Sorcerors weren't noted for their leniency. If he'd
damaged that which he was supposed to safeguard, his
fate would be grim, indeed. He screwed up his courage
and walked across the dead grass to where the jug lay.

Its plug had come out. From the mouth of the jar
issued a thick blue vapor, swirling and thickening before
Fost's eyes. He blinked. A vagrant breeze scattered the
mists momentarily. Then they coalesced into a thin
spire rising directly from the jar.

Dancing motes of energy appeared in the center of
the vapor column, almost too faint to be seen. Whirl-
ing like a miniature tornado, the mist achieved its final
form. Before the startled courier stood the likeness of
a man, tall and thin and aquiline of feature. It smiled
at him benignly, almost beatifically.

"Who . . . ?"

"I am Erimenes the Ethical." The spirit introduced
itself with a bow. "Dead these past one thousand, three
hundred ninety-nine years, but still in possession of my
awesome mental powers."

"Erimenes the Ethical?" Fost touched his jaw with a thumb. "The name strikes a chord in my mind, but . . ."

"Lowborn and ill-educated as you are, you cannot call up the proper referents. But yes, even such as you has heard of me." The spirit sounded pleased.

"You seem to know who I am, but the only Erimenes I can recall is an old philosopher famed for unpopular beliefs."

"Yes," sighed the spirit. "I espoused a monastic philosophy entailing abstinence and the avoidance of all earthly pleasures."

"I can see how that would be unpopular." Some of Fost's courage was returning.

"The centuries spent in that miserable jug convinced me of the error of my tenets. Abstinence, I now feel, should be enjoyed only in moderation. And without excess there can be no moderation." A zephyr made the figure waver. "My time as a shade has not been wasted, my brawling young friend. No, it hasn't. You will be pleased to hear that Erimenes the Ethical now preaches nothing but hedonism."

Nothing remained of Fost's fear. He was confronted by a ghost, true, but a spirit so garrulous hardly proved a menace.

"Isn't it somewhat late to change your views? After all, you've been dead fourteen hundred years."

"One thousand, three hundred ninety-nine," the sage corrected. "But yes, of course, you are right. Without corporeal being, I am nothing. It is regrettably impossible for a vaporous spirit such as myself to enjoy the pleasures of the flesh. Not directly."

"What do you mean?" Fost asked, frowning.

"I merely point out the obvious. A shade must garner whatever sensations it requires vicariously."

Fost realized the source of the mysterious comments last night during the height of his passion with Eliska.

"You mean you're no more than a long-dead voyeur?"

"Really, young man, that puts it so crudely."

"How else would you put it?"

"Let us say I am interested in accumulating experience of the carnal delights in which you revel. Since I sipped not of the sweet wine of youth in life, I may now only look on as others freely quaff."

"Do you mean," Fost asked incredulously, "that you're a virgin? A fourteen-century-old innocent?"

The spirit seemed to blush. "Really, now . . ."

Fost guffawed. "A bedroom-peeper and a virgin! A fine ghost you are, Erimenes. Erimenes the Ethical, indeed!"

The spirit sniffed and turned. Fost laughed uproariously, slapping his muscular thighs in mirth. His earlier fears of Erimenes's bodiless voice amused him now. Kest-i-Mond had gotten a bad bargain when he purchased the jar containing the philosopher's soul.

At length the big man's laughter died down and the shade turned back to face him. "Well," Erimenes said irritably, "I certainly cannot expect someone like you to understand the finer points of my philosophy. Still, you are ideal for my purposes. Your undercover talents are considerable. At least, Eliska was favorably impressed. And the way you dispatched those ruffians in the street was exemplary."

"You saw all that?" asked Fost suspiciously.

" 'Saw' isn't precisely the term, but I would not wish to confuse you with the metaphysical details of how I perceive the world of the living. Suffice it to say I was witness to your exploits in battle as well as bed."

The mist-stuff of the spirit thickened and swirled, and the faint motes of light glowed more brightly. Fost stepped back involuntarily. It took him several seconds to realize the sage was showing his excitement at the thought of killing and wenching.

"I feel we will all be better off when I deliver you to the hand of Kest-i-Mond," he said a bit unsteadily. The spirit looked surprised and opened its mouth as if to protest. Fost swooped down on the lid of the jar, jamming it tightly back into place. The look of surprise and the pale, ascetic face beneath it faded into nothingness as the wind scattered the remnants of the ghostly body.

From inside the jar came a whining complaint. "You didn't have to act so precipitously. I mean you no ill. I only wish to taste, to feel, to know through you the pleasures I denied myself when living."

Ignoring him, Fost walked back to the sled and his patiently waiting dog team. He tossed the jar into the air several times and caught it. A grin spread across his face at the sounds of motion sickness that came from within.

High above, in the bright blue sky, a raven wheeled and cursed Fost Longstrider for a meddling fool. Did the courier somehow suspect the nature of his cargo? But, perhaps, the spirit in the earthenware jar would reveal nothing of its true worth to Kest-i-Mond and the raven's mistress.

The bird quaked at the thought of the sorceress in her high tower. She would not respond well when she learned that Fost knew of the existence of Kest-i-Mond's tame wraith.

Hundreds of feet below, Fost recapped the jar.

Oh, that my hearing were as keen as my sight! the bird lamented. *Then I would know what the long-strider has learned.* It wheeled and headed south.

Its sharp eyes searched the terrain for the small stone

cairn that marked the campsite of its mistress's men-at-arms. The ground grew rockier, irregular stands of trees dotting the countryside. The marker was invisible from the ground, but the raven soon picked out the sparkle of the stacked quartz and pyrite stones and began to spiral downward.

With a quick beat of its wings it killed all forward momentum and alighted on the cairn. It cawed loudly. In less than a minute, a soldier appeared from a dense copse a bowshot distant.

"You have information of value?" the man demanded. A long scar ran from the corner of his eye to his jaw.

The raven croaked in irritation. Humans could be so vexing. Why would it come, if it didn't have something to impart?

"The courier is but an hour's ride hence," it said in its thick-tongued voice. "He carries the vessel you failed to obtain last night."

"It was not *our* failure," rapped the scar-faced officer. "Those were groundlings hired by our Cloud Mistress. *We* shall not fail."

The raven flapped its wings. "You have not seen this man Fost. He is death incarnate to your kind. But I weary of this stilted man-speech. Go now and seize the jar for our mistress."

The scar became a red line down the man's cheek. "We do not take our orders from the likes of you," he said harshly. "For our *mistress* we shall triumph!"

The bird shook its head, smoothed the feathers of its left wing with its beak, and took to the air. Let the foolish one discover for himself how deadly his quarry could be. The raven only observed. Better to report failure, onerous as that duty was, than be the author of that failure.

* * *

The sled rolled smoothly along the road. Since the days of the Empire, upkeep of the Realm Roads had been spotty, but the surface of this highway lay smooth and even. That was one thing that could be said for Count Marll. He attended well to his roads, if not his wife.

The jar in which the spirit of Erimenes the Ethical dwelt was strapped once more to the sled frame. Remembering the way the ghost spied on him the night before, Fost had been tempted to let him bounce around in his jug until he wished he'd never achieved ghostly immortality. The dictates of his profession overrode temptation. Best to deliver his charge to Kest-i-Mond in the best possible condition. An angered enchanter is no one's friend.

He pondered what the departed sage had told him. From his youth in High Medurim he recalled snatches of conversation heard when he stood and begged for bread outside the great seminaries. Erimenes's philosophy of self-denial had enjoyed its popularity—if that was the word—ten centuries ago, but there were still a number of monastic cults devoted to following the master's doctrine.

If only the faithful could see their master now!

Personally, Fost couldn't see the appeal of self-denial. To do without tall flagons of ale and warm, full-bodied wantons to share his bed . . . he shook his head. Life was too soon ended by Hell Call. He could understand the philosophical arguments in favor of abstinence—but look where it had gotten Erimenes. He had life everlasting, true, but it was a pallid thing, lifeless. If that was the cost of immortality, Fost would gladly face the demon of death when the time came and die with a last defiant shout of laughter.

A high-pitched yelp of warning from Wigma made him alert. Instinctively Fost looked over the traces and harnesses, but they were free of fouling. Raissa echoed her mate's cry. Fost looked back along the road.

A cold lump settled in his belly. Dust grew in a spume from the highway perhaps a mile behind: half a dozen men on battle mounts, if Fost read the dust aright. They could not be couriers in such numbers. And travelers rarely ventured so near the Southern Wastes this near the end of the warm season. That left one possibility.

Brigands.

"On! Faster!" Fost cracked his short lash, urging the dogs to greater speed. He had no hope of outracing the long-limbed battle mounts, fierce dogs so huge they could carry an armored man, but he could try to tire them. His sled team had far more endurance than the war-dogs.

The cloud came closer as the minutes raced past. His dogs breathed hard, straining in their harnesses. His pursuers' mounts were fresh, while his animals were wearied from a half-day's travel. His tactic had failed.

He thrust a heavy boot into the dirt and slewed the sled off the road toward a clump of *ofilos* trees. On rough terrain the riding-dogs could still outrun his team, but amid the heavy-limbed trees and tangled brush he'd have a better chance of eluding his enemies.

"What in the name of the Three and Twenty Wise Ones of Agift are you doing?" cried Erimenes from his jug.

"We've got bandits after us. I'm trying to evade them."

·"Bandits?" Erimenes said hopefully. "Why not stop and fight them? You're a skilled bladesman. That was a splendid display in that alley last night. Such strength and skill, such shedding of blood."

"Have done. To fight one man or even three, yes, that may be done. But six or more? Sheer madness!"

"But you cannot flee! That would be cowardice."

"Easy for you to say, who are already dead."

"I long to experience the death-throes of your enemies, the triumph on your face as you slay them. Do you not feel a special thrill when you spill a foeman's lifeblood? Don't your sexual desires soar?"

Fost tried to ignore the spirit as he guided his sled between the silent trees. Here in the forest the dog riders couldn't all attack him at once. He drove the team at a desperate speed.

The headlong race ended when a dog put a foot down a small animal's burrow. The impetus of the sled snapped its leg. The dog fell with a howl and instantly entangled the harness.

Cursing, Fost leaped off the runners and bent over the animal. "You have been a faithful companion, Balf," he said, stroking the matted fur of the dog's head. "Now I must do my duty to you."

A quick slash of his knife sent blood gushing from the dog's throat to soak into the thick carpet of dead leaves. Fost hacked the corpse free of the harness and yelled to the dogs to move on. He jumped onto the sled as it went by, leaving Balf silent and cooling on the ground.

With a gap in the team, Raissa and Wigma redoubled their efforts, and the other dogs followed their example. The sled flew across the slippery, leaf-clad earth. The dogs' panting, the thumping of their paws, the creak and jingle of the harness resounded in Fost's ears.

"Fight!" Erimenes shouted. "Do you wish the rogues to think you craven? Surely you are able to defend yourself."

It was no time to explain the realities of mortal combat to the sage.

"Don't you want to be delivered to Kest-i-Mond?" Fost asked, glancing over his shoulder. No pursuers were in sight. "If you're taken, he'll have to pay a handsome price for your return. He'll be wroth with you."

"Pah! Kest-i-Mond wants knowledge only I possess. He will pay any amount for me, and little count the cost. And what matters it to me who claims ownership of the pot in which I reside? What is the nature of ownership? Is it purely possession or . . ."

"No philosophizing on my time, you long-winded wraith. I'm racing for my life. Yours is forfeit these fourteen centuries past."

The sage started to speak. The sled hurtled toward a shaggy-barked tree overhanging the game path the dogs followed. Fost seized the jar and leaped upward to grab a stout limb. With the philosopher's jug in the crook of his arm, he pulled himself up and began climbing the thick, rough trunk.

Green leaves closed about him like a shroud. The footfalls of the war-dogs pounded closer. Fost tried to make himself as small as possible.

"I never believed a man of your abilities would be capable of such a thing," Erimenes cried. "Running from a noble fight!"

"Quiet," Fost snarled. "What's noble about being sliced to bloody ribbons? Be silent, you fugitive from Hell Call!"

The first of the dog riders passed under the tree in hot pursuit of the unoccupied sled. The rider was small and wiry with a black cloak thrown over his deep purple tunic. No mere bandits, these. Fost's heart hammered as he recognized the curved blades and wicked barbed darts of soldiers of the Sky City, the City of Sorcery.

What could the men of the Soaring World want with him?

The only answer was the spirit in the jar. For all his bloodthirstiness and pomposity, Erimenes possessed some secret of enormous value. And these men, like the unknown assailants of the night before, were ready to kill Fost to get it.

He counted four riders. As the fifth went by Erimenes sang out, "Here, up in the tree! Dolts. A plague on you, look up!"

Fost hit the pot with the base of his fist. "What's wrong with you?" he demanded, sotto voce. "He would have heard, had he been nearer."

"I'm trying to save you from years of mental anguish. You should fight. If you don't, your honor will be tarnished. You will turn in your bed at night, worrying that you are less a man."

"In the tree!" came shouts from below. A sixth rider had heard the dead philosopher discoursing. Fost reacted reflexively. He dropped onto the broad back of the battle-mount, landing behind its rider and slitting the man's throat with a quick slash of his dagger.

Fost hurled the dying man from the saddle and tried to get his feet into the stirrups. The dog snarled and reared. Fost fell to the ground. He stood up, only to fall flat once more to avoid a sword cut from the fifth rider.

"See?" Erimenes's jug had fallen and rolled against the bole of the tree, where it lay unharmed. "You *are* capable of heroic feats when properly motivated. You'll thank me for this in the future, mark my words!"

"I'd mark your back with a whip, had you a back," Fost panted. His sword sang from its sheath to engage the dog rider's blade. Broad paws slapped the ground as the others returned. The need for speed took precedence over chivalry; Fost cut the brindled war-dog's legs from beneath it. It fell, frothing and snapping at its injured limbs, and spilling the rider.

Fost gave the soldier Hell Call, then snatched up the dead man's blade and threw it at a charging blue-black dog. It sank to the hilt in the muscular chest. Bloody foam burst from the dog's nostrils. It toppled, pinning its rider's leg.

Fost had no time to finish off the trapped man. The others rushed the courier. He ducked beneath a silver arc of hard-swung steel and drove his left hand upward. The short, broad blade found a sheath in the man's armpit. The dog rider gave a hoarse cry as his mount carried him past, wrenching the dagger from Fost's grip. The dead man tumbled onto the fallen leaves.

"Dismount. Take him afoot." The scar-faced leader reined in and dropped lithely to the ground. His scimitar twitched in the air like a living thing. "From the sides."

If the two Sky City men were dismayed at three of their number dying and another being disabled in such short order, they didn't show it. They advanced on Fost, the officer on the left and the other swinging wide to take him in a pincers movement. Fost smiled grimly. He was determined to kill one before the other fed a foot of cold steel into his back.

"A superb fight! Blood everywhere. A wonderment!" applauded Erimenes. Fost had a momentary urge to smash the jar before he fell. He didn't know if that would dissipate the ancient philosopher's life-essence and send him at last to Hell, but it would be an interesting experiment.

There was no time for that. The black and purple clad riders pushed him back, trying to herd him away from the spirit's jar. They wanted to insure he couldn't pick it up and flee.

Flight was the last thing on Fost Longstrider's mind. He let his opponents set their pattern of slow, inexorable advance. Then he lunged, flicked a scimitar aside with a forehand stroke, and cut through the right-hand man's throat just below the point of his neatly trimmed beard.

As the rider sank down, drowning in his own blood, the officer closed with a tigerish rush. Fost whirled, throwing up his sword in a blocking motion. The movement came too late. The officer brought his blade down in a slash that laid Fost's back open and sent pain shattering through his spine. Fost gasped and fell forward on his face. He lay, unmoving.

The scar-faced officer raised his hand to slay the injured courier. Then he lowered it and turned away. The discipline of the Sky City was absolute. He had been ordered to return to the Floating Realm with the jar and the spirit it contained without delay, and that was what he would do. Secondary concerns, such as the pleasure of gutting the lowborn scum who had slain four of his men, were luxuries he would not allow himself.

Besides, the courier was as good as dead.

The dog rider walked to the tree and picked up the jug. "You, my black-cloaked friend," Erimenes said brightly, "are an excellent swordsman. Tell me, do you enjoy a good tumble in the hay with a handsome wench from time to time? If so, we might become fast friends."

The officer stared down at the jar, perplexed. He had been warned the spirit might prove uncooperative. Nothing had prepared him for Erimenes trying to beg friendship from him.

He was still puzzling over this turn of events when Fost killed him.

The courier came from behind to drive a dagger, taken from a fallen rider, to the crossguard, just below the man's left shoulder blade. The officer gave a small, surprised cough and collapsed bonelessly.

Fost dropped to his knees and shook the jug as hard as he could.

"You double-dealing spirit," he choked. "Why did you betray me? If you weren't already dead, I'd kill you. I call on the Great Ultimate to give you life so that I may reave it away from you again!"

He continued shaking the jug until Erimenes began to cry. The sound of such pure sorrow made Fost stop.

"I am so weak," moaned Erimenes. "This is why I espoused self-denial. I could never cope with temptation. You—you're so strong. You can live life to the utmost!"

He sniffled, and, even half-dead and dazed, Fost wondered how he accomplished it without benefit of a nose.

"I, however, I have become addicted to sensation since my death. I cannot control myself. I must see blood. I must see carousal. I must, I *must!*"

Fost dropped the jar. Dizziness assailed him. He was torn between disgust and pity for the tormented, treacherous spirit. He tore the Sky City officer's cloak into strips and stanched the flow of blood, then sat weakly with his back to a tree. He was as weak as a day-old pup, but he lived. In spite of the odds, he lived.

A moan of pain came to his ears. He looked around. Not far away lay the last dog rider, still pinned under the corpse of his massive dog. *Now,* Fost thought, *we'll learn why Erimenes is so valuable.*

Unable to walk, he crawled on hands and knees. He was not halfway to the pinned man when a raven flapped down from the sky and landed on a black-cloaked shoulder. With a quick peck the bird took out the rider's eye.

A shriek rent the forest. Another peck plucked out the other eye. A final stab of the iron-hard beak penetrated the soldier's brain. He convulsed once and fell back dead.

The raven swiveled its head as only a bird can, and regarded Fost with such malevolence that the courier's nausea turned to fear. It spread its wings and rose skyward. Fost watched it vanish through the canopy of leaves. Then he fainted.

The raven's mood was bleak as it winged westward. The Sky City was its nest, but it was also the lair in which its mistresses's wrath crouched like a waiting beast. The sorceress would be infuriated that six more of her men, Sky City troops this time, not mere hirelings, had failed at such a simple task. The raven wished another could deliver this message.

It beat stolidly through the air. No war-eagles soared out to meet it. Evidently the enchantress had given orders none was to hinder her winged messenger. It flew in an arched window. The brass perch felt cold and alien in its talons. It cawed once at the sight of its mistress sitting in stony silence with an indigo cloak wrapped about her, awaiting its report.

"Mistress of the Clouds," it said, "I bring bad tidings."

"Failure." The word rang coldly, a death sentence.

"Y-yes, Mistress. Fost Longstrider still lives, still possesses the jar you seek."

"My soldiers."

"All dead, Exalted One."

"Just as well. All would have forfeited their lives for permitting this lowborn lout to best them." She crossed her arms beneath full breasts and began to pace the length of the small room. "Fools, all of them, fools! So simple a chore, and yet it ends in abject failure."

"Do not despair, Mistress," the raven said nervously. "This Fost is mighty, indeed, and cunning."

She turned on him, fury brewing in her eyes. "Enough! How *dare* you suggest this scum can flout the power of the Sky City? *How dare you?* Prince Rann expended forty men learning of that amulet and he who carries the knowledge of it locked in a vaporous brain. I personally conjured for long hours with potent scrying spells to find the jug—and my powers are second to none in the Sundered Realm, including my dear sister. And you *dare* tell me a simple courier is able to thwart my plans? Must I leave the Sky City in this hour of unrest? Must I personally do everything? I dare not leave Rann to deal with such things. So I make plans, simple, easily obeyed plans, and they go awry. *My* plans! How dare you fail!" she screeched.

The raven looked into her cobalt eyes and saw its own death. Wings exploded from its sides as it tried to flee out the open window. The enchantress was quicker. A slim finger pointed. Lambent light shot forth and bathed the creature in flames. It screamed once, piteously, and fell to the floor, a cindered, lifeless ruin.

The stench of burned flesh and feathers filled the chamber. The woman turned and stalked from the room without a glance at the body of her messenger. There were plans to be made for securing the shade of Erimenes the Ethical.

And plans, as well, for the death of the man called Fost.

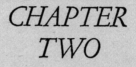

CHAPTER
TWO

A wasp woke Fost by daubing mud in his ear to build its nest. He lay still, too weak to fend off the creature. It soon departed to seek more mud and he rolled over.

Dizziness twisted his senses. He clutched at the moist ground. The spinning died, and Fost struggled to sit up. Agony shot through his back. He reached around to touch the sword cut and regretted it immediately. Pain drew a red curtain before his eyes. "By the Great Ultimate, I hope never to feel this miserable again," he groaned.

"It was your own fault," said Erimenes primly. "Had you fought like a man from the first, you would have won handily. But no, you had to hide and make them ferret you out. You got what you deserved."

"Demons rend you and your sanctimonious prattle," Fost said. "I only want to sleep." He curled up once more, savoring the warmth of sunlight on his aching body. He slept more easily this time.

The setting sun roused him. As he pulled himself upright, he found his hunger nearly as sharp as the pain of his wound. He whistled shrilly, then listened. In a moment he heard the creak of leather and the clinking of the sled's harness. Raissa and Wigma trotted from the dense wood to lap eagerly at his face.

"Old friends," he said shakily, ruffling their fur. "Thank you for standing by me."

He dragged himself to his feet and rummaged through

the foodstuffs packed in the sled. He drew out cloth-wrapped rations. From the dogs' bloodied muzzles, he knew they'd found food for themselves, and indeed there was meat aplenty, harvested by their master's sword arm. He shrugged and began to eat.

The five surviving sled dogs curled up and went to sleep. Finishing his food and washing it down with a swig of brackish water from his canteen, Fost decided a nap was an excellent idea. He lay down between the two lead dogs. While they couldn't compare with Eliska as bedmates, he was in no shape for the activities he'd engaged in with her.

Erimenes's voice woke him with the dawn. "Sluga-bed! Will you sleep away your life? Get up, man, go forth and live. Experience the rich world around you. Fight, love, hate, do something!"

"Demon in a jar," Fost said deliberately, "listen well to me. If ever again you speak unbidden, I'll seek out the deepest crevasse on this planet and heave you into it. I don't have to listen to your words. You're an item to be delivered, and nothing more."

"Nay, I am far more! Locked in my memory is a secret which would cause brother to kill brother, daughter to slay mother. It is—"

"I don't want to hear about it," Fost said with finality. He stood and flexed his powerful limbs. As the blood flowed back into them, he felt the full burden of his weakness. It'd be days before he regained his former strength. Still, with six foes wormfood at his feet, he felt the headiness of victory. The castle of Kest-i-Mond lay but half a day from here. With luck and a bit of caution, he should make it with no further interference. Once at the keep he'd be free of Erimenes and his endless carping. And perhaps then the men of the Sky City would leave him alone.

He dozed intermittently as his dogs paced out the

miles. Occasionally he would stir himself to look for signs of pursuit. None showed in sky or steppe.

The sun had dipped past the zenith when Kest-i-Mond's huge stone and wood pile came into view on the horizon. Fost felt a weight lift from his shoulders.

"Erimenes, old spirit," he said, feeling almost comradely toward the long-dead philosopher, "yonder is your new home. Imposing, isn't it?"

"Utilitarian in the extreme, much as I might have advocated in years past. I should much prefer something more appropriate to my new outlook. A brothel, perhaps."

"I understand Kest-i-Mond lives simply, relishing his privacy. A powerful mage such as he might be able to conjure up something to amuse you."

"In exchange for the secrets I can divulge, he ought to," the spirit said sourly.

"I don't want to hear about your secrets," Fost said. "Only trouble comes to those who learn a sorceror's dark knowledge."

"Rubbish! There is no dark knowledge, merely the layout of a city. It lies in the polar regions. My home," sighed the spirit, "lost these many centuries. Eaten by a glacier."

"Come, Erimenes, a city eaten by a glacier? You make sport of me. A glacier is nothing but a mountainous sheet of ice. I've seen many with my own eyes."

"This is a special glacier," Erimenes said in conspiratorial tones. "Within it lies Athalau, once a mighty city but now dead. A great queen entombed in ice."

"Very poetic." Fost sniffed the air. "*Faugh.* Something reeks. Don't enchanters lime their cesspools?"

"That's sulfur, from the great volcanic activity in this area. The keep was raised in my time by a wizard who kept frequent commerce with the spirits of the inner earth. Perhaps he built it over a fumarole."

"How does Kest-i-Mond stomach the stench?"

"Perhaps he's grown accustomed to it. Now, in Athalau . . ."

Fost shut him out. Let the sage reminisce over his lost city. All Fost wanted was to be rid of him and this treacherous assignment. In the future he would accept only simple tasks. Let the daring venture forth to deal with assassins and eye-plucking ravens.

As for him, he'd take Kest-i-Mond's money and idle away the rest of Count Marll's religious retreat with Eliska. His thoughts turned to the hot-blooded countess. He smiled. And the sage droned on.

The walls of the castle loomed so high they seemed about to topple and crush man and sled alike. In height the keep resembled the buildings of High Medurim, where Fost had been born, but it was all angular and ungainly, with none of the baroque ornamentation popular in the old imperial capital. The odor of brimstone hung in the air, and that, too, brought back Fost's childhood. The sewers ran uncovered in the poorer parts of Medurim.

"End of the line for you, old spirit," he said cheerfully. "I cannot say it's been pleasant knowing you."

"Nonsense. Without me your honor would have been besmirched beyond redemption."

"Never in all my days have I known such a tiresome —hey! What's this?" He jerked the sled to a halt.

"What disturbs you now?" the sage enquired peevishly.

"The doors are ajar." Fost bent and picked up Erimenes's jug. "Strange. I heard Kest-i-Mond was more cautious."

He walked to the bronze doors and peered inside. Nothing stirred. He rapped his knuckles on the doors. They rang hollowly.

"Fost Longstrider, courier, to see the master of the castle."

There was no answer. Fost pushed through the doorway, and the foyer beyond echoed his footsteps. He stood and listened. His heartbeat was the only sound he heard.

He was angry with himself. The philosopher's constant goading had unsettled him. He was growing too wary, almost timid, for fear the bloody-minded shade would precipitate him into another catastrophe. It was only reasonable to feel leery of invading a magician's castle. Still, Fost had legitimate business within the walls of Kest-i-Mond's keep. And an enchanter was just a man, after all, his spells no more than peculiarly potent weapons.

"This vestibule is of no interest to me," Erimenes said. The sound of his dry voice booming in the hallway caused Fost to jump. "Why don't you move on, there's a good lad."

"Shut up! You scared me half out of my wits."

"Little enough to do."

The corridor veered right. Fost followed it, trying to stifle a growing sense of unease. At least he detected no trace of the unpleasant sulfur stink in here. The mage must have spells to freshen his air.

Fost halted. His hand dropped to his sword hilt.

"You sense danger!" Erimenes cried. "What is it? Why do you fondle your weapon?"

"Hold your tongue, if you have one." Fost pointed at the floor in front of them. A dark green marble pedestal lay tumbled on its side, the white bust of a human head in fragments around it. "That's what troubles me."

"Debris. What does it signify?"

"Kest-i-Mond has a fetish for order. It's legendary. In Kara-Est a courtier rearranged the mage's personal effects when he was there on a visit, as a jest. Kest-i-Mond was not amused; he turned the man into a pig. Those who'd enjoyed sexual congress with him were likewise transformed. Fifteen ladies and three squires ended their days in the duke's swineyards."

"A touching story, I'm sure," Erimenes said, "but how does this relate to our dawdling in this dreary hallway?"

"The door open, a statue shattered on the floor—these indicate the presence of uninvited guests, do they not?" He drew his sword.

He scanned the passageway. A dark stain on the stone floor caught his eye. He bent over and sniffed it.

"Blood. And not human blood, if I'm any judge. The color's wrong, as well as the smell."

The purplish pool trailed off into an alcove. Fost stepped cautiously to the archway. His gorge rose.

Had the thing in the alcove been alive Fost would have cried out in fear. But it was very, very dead. It had been a monster with the head and upper torso of a muscular man, slimming to the hips to become the thick, powerful tail of a giant serpent. Its throat was disfigured by huge blue weals like the marks of mis-shapen fingers. Its head had been pounded to a pulp.

"Intruder? Or guardian of the way?" Sweat beaded on Fost's forehead, though the corridor was cool. "Either way, someone's been here before us. Finding Kest-i-Mond takes on greater urgency."

"Why trouble Kest-i-Mond?" Erimenes asked. "He's obviously lost interest in me, or he would have been at the door to take delivery. Let's return to Kara-Est. It's a seaport; you can guide me through the fleshpots. They should prove quite diverting."

"Are you never quiet? I accepted the commission to deliver you to Kest-i-Mond. I cannot forsake my duty as a courier, nor am I about to risk an enchanter's wrath merely to satisfy your unnatural tastes. I've been damned near cut in two trying to deliver you, and deliver you I will!"

"I hardly expected to find you so humorless."

"If I don't find Kest-i-Mond, I don't get paid. I want *some* recompense for getting cut up and having to listen to you. I . . ." He stopped. His ears had sensed a slight rustling, as if a mouse hastened to its hole. He knew no mage would permit mice to run freely in his keep; a simple spell banished vermin. A flicker of movement in another archway snared his gaze.

A reverberating roar filled the corridor. A great, shaggy, reeking form rushed from the arch and blundered into a wall. Bellowing with rage, it turned toward the courier.

Fost backpedaled, keeping his sword at *garde*. Facing him was an immense apelike creature with long fur striped brown and black. The upper half of its face was blackened ruin, as though blasted by a bolt of lightning. Below its blinded eyes and flat, wide-nostriled nose was a loose-lipped mouth filled with vicious yellow fangs.

Blind as it was, Fost knew better than to underestimate it. The monster flexed long-fingered hands and uttered a shrill cry like a cross between a child weeping and a man dying in agony. The stench of the thing put to shame a charnel pit.

"What manner of being is this?" Erimenes asked brightly.

"Blind, you idiot!" hissed Fost. "Don't let it hear you."

"Don't be absurd. You can defeat an injured creature. Go on, attack!"

The ape-thing's lips curled into a ghastly semblance

of a human smile. Its expression sickened Fost more than its smell or its devastated face. Something in that half-human visage mocked his very existence.

He ducked and dodged as a hairy arm groped for him. The creature grinned and slobbered down its chinless face. It struck out again, and Fost saw gobbets of flesh adhering to its filthy nails.

"Really, Fost, this is ridiculous. At least let me out so I may have a decent view. You jostle me around so!"

Fost refused to be goaded into answering. The spirit wanted him to speak and draw the monster's attention. Instead he laid the jar on the floor and slid it away from him. The creature's head turned to track the sound of the pot skittering across the floor and hitting the wall. It let out a gloating growl and leaped.

Fost side-stepped and jammed his sword into its side. Bone deflected his blade, but the sword bit deep. He twisted it and yanked it free. The creature spun on him with an angry snarl.

He slashed at the arms that reached out to draw him into a crushing embrace. The cuts bled fiercely, but seemed to trouble the monster no more than the huge, flowing wound in its side. Fost found himself driven to the wall.

"Enough of this," he mumbled. He took a quick step and lunged. His blade sank into the hairy beast.

The beast wrenched the sword from his grasp by turning, the blade half embedded in its chest.

"By the Dark Ones, will nothing stop you?" Fost threw himself to the side. The hallway resounded as the monster slammed into the wall. Had Fost not moved, the bulk would have smashed him.

He whipped dagger from sheath, more out of habit than because he thought it would do any good. The impact of the ape-creature against the wall had driven

Fost's sword to the hilt in its chest, yet the monster seemed stronger than ever.

"The being, you will be pleased to know, lacks something of substance in this dimension," Erimenes said from his jar.

"What are you talking about? 'Lacks substance'? It nearly pulverized me!"

"It appears to hail from a reality paralleling our own. The fabric of space has been altered to draw it hence, and the transition is only partially complete."

Fost shook his head. His outburst had drawn the apparition's attention to him again. It approached slowly, grinning hideously.

He felt no surprise that the beast was not of this world; an earthly being would have died a dozen times from the wounds it had received.

Fost shouted, then dove past the monster and beneath the sweep of its talon-tipped arms. His dagger bit the back of the monster's knee in passing. It staggered.

By the time it recovered, Fost had rolled to his feet and was pounding down the corridor.

"Coward!" Erimenes's voice rang at his heels. "Stand and fight like a man!"

Up the hall a door yawned. Fost dashed through, shutting it behind him. A massive key jutted from the lock, and he turned it with a sigh of relief. The door was stout oak and surely enough to withstand even the monster in the corridor.

"Fool!" Erimenes's scornful voice echoed faintly through the wood. "That won't do you any good. Fight, fight I say!" Fost closed his eyes and leaned wearily against the door.

And almost died. The monster's arm came *through* the wood and dealt him a vicious blow to the side of the head. He sprawled headlong. Stunned, he turned over to see the ape-thing emerging slowly from the heavy door.

"Great Ultimate!" Fost scrambled to his feet. His head reeled from the blow but he had no time to waste. He forced himself into a brain-jarring run even as the monster came fully into the room.

He jerked open another door and fled through it. Blundering and crashing, the monster followed. He led it a nightmare chase through a maze of rooms and corridors. Slammed doors held it up for scant seconds and, though blinded, it trailed the courier with the grim facility of a tracking dog.

The air grew hot. At first Fost thought it was due to his own exertion, but when he leaned against a wall to catch his breath the stone was hot to the touch.

Perhaps I'm near the scullery, he thought. *There may be a way out of this hellhole.*

He came to another door. It refused to open. From behind sounded a clatter as the monster overturned a table in its haste to reach him.

"Let me in!" Fost shouted, hammering frantically on the wood. "Gods below, open up!" The door stayed shut.

He heard toenails scraping stone. The door shuddered as he threw his weight into it. Long disused, the door had warped until it jammed the frame.

Fost heard the gurgling breath of the monster. He expected at any instant to feel those foul hands close around his neck. He yelled in desperation and lunged full force against the door.

It burst inward in a shower of splinters. Fost lurched into the room beyond. A nose-searing reek of sulfur hit him in the face, and he pulled up short.

It was well that he did so. He looked down. A hand's-breadth beyond the toes of his boots was . . .

nothing. A vast black pit gaped before him. Sulfurous fumes issued from it in thin yellow wisps.

He flattened himself against the warm, sulfur-encrusted wall beside the door.

"Come on," he called. "Come and take me, you bastard spawn of hell!"

With a roar of triumph, the monster charged the open door. Straight over the brink it ran. For a moment it hung in air, clawing at nothingness. Then it dropped from view.

Fost pushed off from the wall and peered down the hole. The fumes made his eyes water. The ape-thing had been swallowed by unfathomable darkness. The courier heard it bellow once, faintly; then all was silence.

He backed from the room, bent double, gripping his knees and gasping for breath. Gradually his strength returned as the aftermath of fear subsided. When he felt more fully himself he went in search of Erimenes. After his experience with the monster, even the company of the verbose spirit was preferable to being alone.

"I'm bored with searching," the philosopher said. "Let's go and find some winsome lass. Perhaps two. Yes, a fine idea, as fine as ever I've had."

"I'm glad you think so," Fost said dourly.

"Really, Fost, your unimaginative adherence to what you conceive to be your duty astonishes me. If Kest-i-Mond cared whether he got me or not, he wouldn't have left us to wander about this drafty castle all afternoon."

"Dark Ones! I must find the enchanter, if only to learn why I am beset by brigands, dog riders and devils," Fost said. "Besides, how do you know it's drafty? You're in a jar."

"True. But it looks drafty."

They came to a stairway. Fost peered up. "I think I've found something," he said.

A corpse, charred to a grotesque doll, sprawled on the steps before them.

"This changes things!" Erimenes' voice rang with delight. "Press on, press on. Battle may await us."

"Grand." Despite his own misgivings, Fost mounted the stair. He kicked the burned body from his path. An arm broke off and tumbled down the stairs. He shuddered and started to climb.

A sword lay on the steps. It was short, curved, keen of blade—Sky City workmanship. Fost sighed. He picked up the weapon, tried unsuccessfully to fit it into his straight scabbard, and finally thrust it under his belt. His own sword had gone into the pit with the monster, still embedded in its breast.

He climbed higher up the spiraling stairs. They came upon another body, burned into two pieces. Further up was a corpse with its head and shoulders cindered beyond recognition. The bodies wore the all-too-familiar purple and black of the City in the Sky.

In all, Fost passed seven corpses on the long, tiring climb. Whatever magic Kest-i-Mond had employed had proven effective. He recalled the way the ape-creature's face had been blasted and burned.

But not effective enough, he thought.

Erimenes seemed to read his thoughts. "Fortunate for you that you came across the fumarole. If Kest-i-Mond's death-bolts did not slay the monster, you would have fared poorly. Still," he sighed, "what a fight it would have been."

A brass-bound door barred their way. Fost kicked it open, his sword held ready. The light of the setting sun streamed in a narrow window to fill the cramped room like melted butter.

"Your purchaser has indeed lost interest in you," Fost said. "He has heard the Hell Call." At his feet lay the body of a frail, ancient man. His head had been turned around on his neck so that his dead face studied the uncaring stone floor of the chamber.

The room had been ransacked. There seemed to have been no purpose to the destruction. Benches were over-turned, phials of powder and noxious-looking fluids smashed, a case of scrolls cast down, all at random. Fost surmised that the monster, blinded by the sor-ceror's spell, had broken Kest-i-Mond's neck and vented its rage by tearing the room apart.

"*Now* can we repair to some house of ill repute?" Erimenes asked. "I desperately need some diversion after the dreary miles we've walked today."

"*I* walked," Fost corrected. "You rode." He exam-ined the relics scattered about the floor. Against one wall lay a tiny ebony bowl chased with silver and covered with a tight-fitting lid. He set the jug down and picked up the bowl.

"Fair workmanship," he appraised. "Not much in the way of booty, but it looks to be all the payment I'll get for this ill-starred mission." Nearby sat a chalice of sim-ilar design. He put the bowl in his pouch and picked up the cup. On impulse he pulled off its cover and watched in surprise as it filled with clear liquid. He took a sip, spat it out. "Water. Tepid water, at that."

"Kest-i-Mond appears to have had simple tastes," Erimenes said. "I prefer being with you. A brawling young buck who knows how to *live*. Yours is the kind of existence I want to observe."

Fost prodded the corpse with his toe. It rolled onto its side. A scrap of parchment stuck out from under the body. He bent to retrieve it.

"What have we here? A map, a sorcerous one, by the look of it." His brow wrinkled as he studied it, tracing

outlines that glowed with a silvery light of their own.
"Old High Imperial script—this must be a thousand
years old! The steppes, Samadum, the Southern Waste
and the . . . what's this? Here, south of the Rampart
Mountains in the polar lands. What does this circle
mean?"

Erimenes did not reply.

Fost eyed the jug suspiciously. "Speak to me. You've
filled the air with words whenever it was least convenient for me. This map is old and valuable. Any
artifact with scriptsilver is worth a king's ransom.
What does it mean?"

"I know nothing that would be of use to you."

"You're lying. You started before to tell me of your
home in the south. 'Eaten by a glacier,' you said. There's
a glacier marked within this circle. Is this why Kest-i-
Mond wanted you?"

"Yes."

"You're reticent for once. What secret does this city
hold? Why do armed men and a netherworld demon
invade a mage's castle? Why do minions of the City
in the Clouds seek to wrest you from me at every
turn?"

"How should I know this? I weary of your tirade.
Let's go to Kara-Est or perhaps back to Samadum.
Eliska awaits you—and the white circle of her
arms. . . ."

"Enough! Speak to me of your long lost home. Tell
me about Athalau."

"You remember the name. I commend you."

"And I'll give you to the Josselit monks if you don't
tell me what you would have revealed to Kest-i-Mond."

"The Josselit monks?" quavered the spirit.

"You know of them, surely. Their philosophy is one
you would heartily have approved of—once. Abstinence
from the pleasures of the flesh and the company of

women. Bread soaked in salt water and a cup of vinegar each day." Fost grinned hugely. "Of course, once a year, or so I'm told, they cease their prayers and indulge in a solemn play about the Five Holy Ones. You'll love the Josselits, Erimenes."

"Your jest is in extremely poor taste."

"It's no jest. Keep your secret to yourself and soon there will be none but monks to hear it."

There was a lengthy pause which Fost enjoyed immoderately. He knew the spirit would answer. Nor did Erimenes disappoint him.

"Very well," sniffed the shade. "I never realized the streak of cruelty ran so deep in you. In Athalau is the Amulet of Living Flame. Evidently, Kest-i-Mond desired it."

"Go on. What is this amulet, that so many have died because of it?"

"A mere bagatelle. Clasp it to your breast as you die and you escape Hell Call."

"You live again?"

"Exactly. The sorcerors of my city know many potent magics. Before the glacier consumed Athalau, the Amulet of Living Flame was considered a mere trinket compared to others, which imparted great wisdom, the power over fickle chance, overwhelming inner peace. Only the sorcerors of the Sky City have ever approached the skill of the Athalar."

"To cheat death." The words tasted good.

"Yes, that is what the amulet does, if it hasn't crumbled to dust."

"What!"

"The power tends to drain from a magical item as the centuries pass," Erimenes explained. Then, as if in afterthought, he added, "I doubt this to be the case with the Amulet of Living Flame, though."

"Why not?" Fost almost shouted.

"Its property of storing the life-energy to restore it to the deceased individual, of course. Some little accrues to the amulet with each usage. Such would tend to preserve it, or so I suspect. These sorcerous matters are outside my province, you understand."

"To defy the demon of death," Fost breathed. "That is a trinket worth fighting for."

"Indeed," said Erimenes carefully. "Many a glorious battle would have to be fought to obtain the amulet. All in vain, of course. Even with the map to guide you, you could never get into the city in the glacier. And if you could, you'd never locate the amulet." He paused. "Not unless you took me along to guide you, as Kest-i-Mond intended to do."

"Done!" cried Fost. He caught up the jar and ran down the stairs, his feet barely touching the cold stone. A treasure more precious than any hoard of gold or jewels beckoned him southward.

The promise of everlasting life.

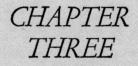

CHAPTER THREE

A breeze shifted the limbs of the big tree. Fost snorted in his sleep and half-turned. His perch threatened constantly to dump him to the ground fifteen feet below, and the hard, rough limbs could never be mistaken for a sumptuous down mattress. Despite the draft and the discomfort, he slept soundly.

Once, in the forests above Port Zorn, a magician's apprentice had hidden his scent under a sorcerous potion and crept past Fost's dogs to within reach of the courier's bedroll. Fost never knew what sense it was that saved him. Abruptly, his eyes had opened and the apprentice's sickle was a yellow arc of moonlight curving for his throat. He had rolled to the side, the curving blade cutting deep into the soft ground. Fost had slain his attacker with an underhand dagger toss.

Since then he'd learned to sleep with a healthy distance between him and the ground. Raissa and Wigma were incomparable watchdogs, but even they could be fooled.

He moved his shoulders in an unconscious effort to ease the pressure of the wood against his body. He hadn't lashed himself in place, since that tended to cut off circulation. His scimitar hung in easy reach, looped through his belt and dangling from a nearby branch.

As he slept, he smiled. His dreams were pleasant. Eternal life! The very thought that he alone in all the world had the secret of the Amulet of Living Flame's location filled him with a warm, triumphant glow. He'd not been paid gold for his troubles in delivering Erimenes to Kest-i-Mond, but a vastly greater reward seemed just within his reach.

Old Gabric, his employer back in Tolviroth Acerte, would take a dim view of one of his couriers going absent without leave. And whenever delivery of an item was impossible there were explanations to be made and forms to be filled out in bushel-loads. The Dark Ones take Gabric and his forms in triplicate! With the amulet in his hand, Fost would be as far above such concerns as the Sky City was above the plains and mountains of the Quincunx.

Eternal life! He would outlive his enemies, gain new ones, outlive them as well. Sword cuts would heal instantly; disease could gain no hold in his body; he could quaff poison like clear spring water. He would be unkillable.

His ambition did not stop there. Since his days as a starving guttersnipe in High Medurim, he'd had a hunger for knowledge. He'd taught himself to read ancient scripts and spent what time he could poring over books of science, history, philosophy. But the hard life of a courier left little time for such luxury. With the amulet, though, all of time would be his. He could exhaust the Imperial Library at Medurim with its nine million volumes; he could become the most knowledgeable man in creation. With his strong sword arm and his mind filled with a hundred centuries of human wisdom, he might become invincible.

He sighed. A dream fluttered pleasantly across his mind: himself and a voluptuous black-haired woman whiling away eternity in an unending assortment of passionate embraces. He'd drunk the lukewarm water from Kest-i-Mond's magic chalice, and filled his belly with the equally uninspired gruel provided by the covered bowl. Now his sleeping mind turned its attention to other appetites not so recently sated.

Then he was sailing through the air.

For a second he thought his erotic dream had taken flight. The ground slammed him with the impact of a falling building, and his breath exploded from his lungs.

His still-healing body felt as if it had cracked all over like a pot dropped on pavement. He lay still while bright lights danced behind his eyes. He fought to regain his wind. Vivid in his mind was the impression of strong fingers grasping his ankle the instant before he fell.

"What's this?" Fost heard Erimenes ask. The intruder's clothes rasped bark as he slithered down the tree, carrying Fost's pouch with the philosopher inside. "Most foully done! How can you have a rousing duel with one of the participants stunned?"

The intruder hissed at the spirit to be silent. Fost got his arms under him and pushed his leaden body off the ground, intending to snare the thief's leg as he went by. A footfall thumped the springy earth nearby and lightning split Fost's skull as the thief smashed his sword's pommel down on top of Fost's head.

Fost's face slammed into the dirt, but he didn't lose consciousness. He lay a moment while his stomach performed remarkable acrobatics, then he raised his head, spat out a mouthful of dead leaves and shouted, "Up, Wigma, Raissa! Rend him!"

Silence greeted his shout, broken only by the muffled steps receding into the forest. It occurred to him that his sled team had given no warning of the intruder's presence. He climbed to his feet, an effort akin to scaling a sheer cliff with large rocks strapped on his shoulders. For a few ragged breaths he stood propped against the tree, fighting nausea and the blinding ache in his head.

Then he dragged himself laboriously up the trunk to retrieve his sword.

The climb almost exhausted him, but he had no intention of going after an armed opponent with no weapon of his own, particularly in this condition. Nor did he intend to allow the sneak-thief to escape with Erimenes. He wouldn't be robbed this easily of eternal life!

He set out in the direction his attacker had taken. He passed his dogs, who lay still, dead or unconscious. That explained why no warning had been given.

It was far too dark and the tumult in his skull too great to allow him to track the thief by sight. But the crack on the head seemed to have sharpened his hearing. Pausing, he heard a faint, familiar voice say, "Wait, How can you run so cravenly? You're as bad as Fost!"

Despite the agony in his head, he smiled grimly. For once the spirit's garrulity was disrupting someone else's plans. It was high time.

He followed the sound. True to form, Erimenes was berating the thief at the top of his voice, demanding that he turn back immediately and fight like a man. Fost hoped the thief would be distracted by the spirit's chatter. In his condition, he only had one strong sword thrust in him, and he had to make it good.

He all but stumbled across the thief. The cloaked form had stopped in a small clearing and stood shaking the pouch with both hands, cursing at Erimenes to be silent. Though his sword felt as if it weighed ten pounds, he swung it with a strength fed by fury.

The scimitar's tip brushed a low-hanging branch. The thief spun away like a cat. A straight, slim length of steel quickly glittered in the starlight between the dark-cloaked form and Fost.

"Pah!" jeered Erimenes. The thief had dropped him

to the ground. "Such a clumsy stroke. My new friend will show you skill!"

Perhaps he would. It was taking most of Fost's strength simply to stay upright. The confident, easy stance of his foe spoke eloquently of skill. Fost couldn't afford to fence with the thief.

The intruder twitched his sword tip in tight patterns in the air, hoping to snare Fost's gaze. The instant that happened the blade would straighten and stab unerringly through the courier's heart. Fost took a deep breath. Roaring, he beat aside the thief's sword and charged like a rogue bull. His body collided with the other as the straight sword cartwheeled away. A shrill, angry squeal burst from his foe's lips and shocked him like a blow.

His opponent was a woman!

They went down in a tangle. "Ground-born lover of goats," the women snarled. "I'll cut out your liver and make you eat it!"

She eeled out of Fost's arms and tried to get up. His own sword had fallen from his grip. He seized her by a trim calf and brought her crashing down. Erimenes was cheering wildly, but for which of the combatants Fost couldn't tell.

He pulled himself atop the woman, striving to pin her with his greater weight. Her fingers clawed his face and sought his eyes. She brought her knee up hard. He stopped it with his thigh but in turning slipped off the writhing body.

They rolled over and over, grappling, struggling for advantage. Fost was weakened by wounds and his fall, and the woman's muscles seemed wound from steel wire. But Fost had grown up on the hard tenement streets of High Medurim and he knew all there was to know about vicious rough-and-tumble fighting before he reached his teens. After a few panting, cursing minutes, he lay on top of her limp body, trapping her arms at her sides.

For a time he could do no more than lie there. His head reeled and his body cried from a hundred aches. His face was thrust into the juncture of shoulder and slim neck, his cheekbone pressed to hers to keep her from turning to bite him.

Gradually his sickness subsided. He became aware of the scent of her crisp, clean hair. He'd been sleeping with his tunic unlaced, and the garment had been partially torn from him in the fight. Disturbingly, his bare chest touched equally bare feminine skin.

Without moving he swiveled his eyes down. The clasp holding her cloak had opened and ripped a long rent in her jerkin. Her breasts were naked, crushed by his powerful chest, and he realized in amazement that the nipples were poking solidly into his flesh.

He raised himself slowly, ready for the explosion of movement as the thief tried to escape. It didn't come. She lay on her back, eyes closed, lips slightly parted and her full, pale breasts rising and falling with the cadence of her breathing. The nipples were dark as wine, and jutted from coppery aureoles shaped like dainty mushroom caps.

He closed his eyes. Unbidden came the memory of his dream of Eliska. This wench was as lovely as Eliska, and the fullness of her body covered an athletic musculature the pampered countess could never hope to match. It had been long days since Eliska, too long.

His eyes opened. She was looking up at him. The night turned her eyes dark, but they showed green highlights in the shimmer of the stars. Her tongue peeked out to make a slow circuit of her lips.

She squirmed an arm free. He let her. She lifted a

long, fine hand and stroked her forefinger down his chest.

"You are strong," she said. Her voice was husky, but not from exertion or fear.

Erimenes spoke. Fost never heard him. The thunder of blood in his ears drowned out all sound as his arms circled the woman and his face came down to hers. She raised her head and boldly met his kiss. Her tongue slipped into his mouth. His twined around it slowly. He felt the sweet tension build in the luscious body trapped beneath his own. Pain and tiredness ebbed magically from him.

He laid a scarred hand on her breast. Her hands slid down on his hips to tug at his breeches. He tilted his body off hers, squeezing the nipple between his fingers as he did so, and tangled his other hand in her golden hair. He sighed as her cool fingers wrapped around his manhood and tugged it free.

She undulated beneath him as she shed her own breeches. Their mouths were still joined, lip to lip, tongue to tongue, salivas mingling to form a heady wine. Her legs spread in wanton invitation; the sweet perfume of her body enveloped him like an aphrodisiac. He lowered his body slowly, gliding into her.

Her arms twined around his neck. She drew him down into a long, fervent kiss as he thrust into her with a steady pressure. She drew in a breath, tightening herself around him like a noose. His fingers kneaded her back. Fire flared within his loins. He withdrew, meaning to make his lovemaking slow, but her hips began a slow circle and he lost all control.

Her fingers ran up and own his back like tiny animals as he plunged in and out. The thief dug her heels into the carpet of the mulch and gave him back stroke for stroke. Her femininity devoured him as Fost ground his chest against her breast.

Air hissed from the woman's flaring nostils; his breath came in short gasps. Her fingers clawed in frenzy at his back. Pain shot through him as they raked the half-healed sword cut, but then his body yielded to the sweet insistency. The pain went far away as ecstasy washed over his senses.

Passion subsided into gentle languor. Their mutual death grip eased. Fost let himself slip to one side. Her eyes were half-lidded, her breath warm on his lips. She kissed him once, unspeaking, and closed her eyes.

Weariness settled over him like a blanket. He had pushed himself too far, too fast. Though instinct told him he should be shaking the woman roughly awake to demand who she was and why she wanted to steal the spirit in the jug, nature demanded rest. Instead he slept, his arms locking the slender woman tightly to him.

His arms still circled the naked woman when he awoke. The forest was dark, but overhead birds sang to greet the first pink touches of dawn in the eastern sky. The cool air washed his body, which seemed one enormous ache. The lovemaking of the night before had been hot delight, but it hadn't done his physical condition any good.

His stomach grumbled. His mouth felt as if it were stuffed full of cotton. Food and drink seemed in order. He disentangled his arms from the sleeping woman, and winced at the twinge from the slash the Sky City officer had given him across the back a few days ago. She opened her eyes. They were brilliant green in the growing light.

"Good morning," she said. Her voice was low and lilting, and despite her sleepy muzziness it was as lovely a voice as he'd ever heard. He smiled and brushed black hair from his eyes.

"And to you, thief."

"Moriana," she said. "My name is Moriana." She sat up and thrust her arms high above her head and stretched like a waking cat. He watched the play of muscles across her belly and up her arms. The sun's first rays turned the thatch between her thighs to fine golden wire. She arched her back, conscious of his attention. Her high breasts flattened against her ribs.

Fost tried to sort out his feelings toward the lovely thief. She'd come within a hair of robbing him of his chance at eternal life—she'd come close to robbing him of life, period. But then it somehow changed, and she had been feigning nothing when she gave herself to him. It was as if each had seen in the other some sign that changed them from adversaries into something he could not yet put a name to.

"Moriana, then," he said, yawning widely. "What made you decide to take up thievery?" He fumbled in the satchel containing Erimenes and found the bowl and chalice he'd taken from Kest-i-Mond's study. He casually tossed aside Erimenes's jar, hoping to infuriate the spirit. The shade remained uncharacteristically quiet.

Moriana shrugged. It made her bare breasts bobble enticingly. "I've little enough choice," she said sadly. "I've neither money nor birth. If I want to survive out on the road, I must steal, or . . ." Her words trailed off, but the meaning was clear.

Fost said nothing. The state of his belly occupied his full attention. He drank from the cup, looked across its rim at Moriana, and handed it to her. She sipped as he uncovered the bowl and began to spoon up gruel. The thin porridge was as unappetizing as ever, but it was preferable to the cavernous emptiness in his stomach.

"Thank you," she said, setting down the cup. She tilted her head and smiled. "Whomever you may be."

"Fost Longstrider. I'm a courier." He spooned up the last of the gruel, made a face at the tasteless stuff as the bowl began to fill again. He proferred it. "Do you want some? There's plenty, the gods know."

"It's most courteous of you to feed someone who tried to rob you."

He laughed. "You did rather more than that. Besides, I'm curious. How did you manage to get past my dogs?"

"A small potion I stole from an enchanter. The dogs sniff it and turn drowsy. It's harmless." She paused, lowering her eyes. "I'm sorry."

"You mean you're sorry I caught you?"

"No." Her eyes avoided his. "You're a generous man. You shouldn't be plagued by petty thieves like me."

He stared at her. She seemed to mean it. She made him strangely uncomfortable. He tried to pass it off with a joke. "Petty? Pretty, I'd say." He lifted her chin and smiled.

She reached out, hesitant, and touched his cheek. The slender fingers were supple-skinned and pale. The only trace of marring hardness was the characteristic swordsman's callus on the side of her right index finger.

"You're kind. I knew you were when you didn't kill me last night. Lesser men would have."

"Lesser men would have missed a beautiful experience."

"So would I."

It was his turn to avoid her gaze. "You still haven't told me how you come to be out cutting purses and drugging defenseless animals. Eat, and give me the story. I'd think one so beautiful would long since have married into lands and wealth beyond the dreams of a poor man like myself."

Her cheeks flushed slightly. Modesty? Or something else? It was hard to reconcile her almost virginal attitude with her bold wantonness of the night before. And she made no effort to cover her nakedness.

She was a complex creature, this Moriana. He would enjoy unraveling the mysteries surrounding her.

She hesitated, cast away fastidiousness, and dipped Fost's spoon into the replenished gruel before speaking.

"I cannot marry. I've no dowry; my family is dead, all but my poor sister." She wrinkled her nose at the gruel. "Awful stuff."

"But all we have. And anyway, it's free. Go on."

"It's not a pleasant story. My father was an artisan in Brev, in the Great Quincunx. An evil sorceror lusted after my mother. She spurned him; my father challenged the mage to a duel. The mage slew him. When he came for my mother, she killed herself. So he took my sister, my poor lovely sister, and forced her to be his mistress instead. I was gone from the house, at the market. When I returned . . ." Her voice broke. She dropped the bowl and buried her face against Fost's shoulder, sobbing bitterly. He cradled her, stroking her long hair and murmuring soothing words to her. He found himself once more acutely aware of what an armful she was. His hand dropped to her behind. He snatched it away. This was no time for such things.

She pushed herself away and looked up at him with red-rimmed eyes. "Help me forget," she said. "Help me."

He reached around her and carefully packed bowl and chalice back into the satchel. The tip of one breast lay against his chest. He felt the ripeness of the nipple prodding him. With a deft flick of his wrist, he dropped Erimenes's jug into the satchel and drew the string tight.

Her hands gripped his biceps, shaking. He lay back, pulling her down on top of him. Their bodies twisted demandingly, reliving the passions of the previous night. Afterwards, he slept.

When he awoke, he was alone.

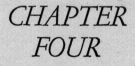

*CHAPTER
FOUR*

Fost rolled over. Pain stabbed through his muscles. He stretched, groaning as joints cracked. Feeling better, he pulled himself to a sitting position and looked around.

The grass around him was crushed, testimony to the passion of the night before. The satchel containing Erimenes, the chalice, and the bowl was gone. Fost lifted a corner of Moriana's cloak, on which he'd lain with the pretty thief. It was fine maroon velvet lined with gold silk. Expensive, plainly—but no compensation for the loss of eternal life.

Fost rose, stood a moment amid the clean, sweet odor of grass, trees and morning, holding the cloak by a corner. He sighed. He leaned down, collected his sword and stuffed it back through his belt, and set off through the woods toward the tree in which he'd begun last night.

A breeze gently sighed through the trees, and a yellow bird sang from a high limb. Retracing the steps that had led him to the clearing was simple. In his fury and urgency, he'd trampled through the undergrowth like a hornbull in rut.

The heavy cloak draped over his shoulder, he came to the tree from which his empty scabbard still dangled. His sled wasn't far away. He saw no signs of his dogs. Putting fingers to lips, he whistled once, twice, three times. In a few minutes, Raissa and Wigma trotted from

the brush side by side, followed by the other three surviving animals of his team. The black and silver bitch
licked bloody froth from her muzzle. She had been hunt-
ing again.

"Do you know that devious witch almost had me
believing her?" he asked his dogs as he knelt to strap
them into the harness. "Even after the clumsy way she
tried to lie to me." He shook his head. "Telling me of
the simple life of toil she'd led when her fingers were
as soft as a maiden's bottom save for a swordsman's
callus. And that fanciful tale about a magician stealing
away her sister—ha! An insult to my intelligence."

Finished, he straightened. His dogs looked up, their
ears cocked to listen attentively, as though comprehend-
ing their master's words. "Nor was her accent that of
Brev-town; and had she been raised in the streets,
she'd have known enough of rough-and-tumble fighting
to make me unfit for our later bout of wrestling." He
sighed again. "Still, she's a rare one. It'll be a pity to
wring her devious neck when I've run her down."

He climbed onto the runners and clucked the dogs
into motion. Steering skillfully among the trees, he
brought the sled to the clearing where he'd awakened.
Halting, he hunkered down by the lead dogs and held
the rich cloak to their noses. They sniffed obediently
and pulled the sled forward to the patch of flattened
grass. Ranar wailed with excitement as he recognized
the thief's odor. Wigma snarled savagely at the
youngster, then lifted a hurt, puzzled face to his master.
The older, wiser dog had already discovered that the
scent they were to follow couldn't be detected outside
the circle of the crushed grass.

Fost laughed. "So she covered her personal scent
with a canthrip. As I knew she would; that spell's hedge-
magic, and I suspect she knows enchantments far more
esoteric." He reached into a pocket of his tunic, pro-

duced a mottled handkerchief redolent of soured gruel, and held it down for his dogs to smell.

Raissa yipped, strained a few feet away from the slept-on patch, smelled the ground, and yipped again. Her mate echoed the call. They'd found a trail.

"On!" Fost shouted, jumping back onto the runners. "Track down that deceitful bitch, and we'll see why she's so eager for Erimenes's company." Guided by their sensitive noses, the team set off through the forest at a brisk trot.

Life in High Medurim's slums allowed few fools to survive to manhood. Short of killing the lovely thief on the spot, there'd been no way to keep her from stealing the jug from him out there in the woods. Hard as he was, Fost had been unable to bring himself to murder Moriana in cold blood, especially after making love to her. He had, however, jammed the lid of the ever-filled gruel bowl open a hair's-breadth with a small pill of pitch, and then made sure the bowl went into the sack with the philosopher's jug. The gruel would seep out in a slow stream, soak through the satchel, and leave a trail for the dogs to sniff along in pursuit.

Confident that the spell hiding her own smell would keep Fost's dogs from tracking her, she was making no other effort to escape detection. He would catch her soon. He wanted to know how she'd learned of Erimenes's existence—and what she intended to do with the sage. He had a suspicion her motives were different from his straightforward lust for immortality.

Immortality. The word rang in his brain. He would not forsake it, no matter the cause for which Moriana might desire the Amulet of Living Flame. The conviction was growing in him that he'd have to kill the beautiful adventuress to get her to give up the idea of using the amulet for her own ends. The thought troubled him strangely.

Whistling to cover his odd discomfort, he rode the sled northward among rapidly thinning trees.

North of the Southern Steppe, the land began to turn green and undulate into high-grassed prairie. Rivers ran down from the mountains of the Thail, branching into myriad streams and brooks. At the bottom of a shallow depression, one such stream had widened into a clear pool. Moriana sat on her haunches beside it, staring intently into the water.

Her gold hair hung to her shoulders, stirred now and then by a stray breeze wandering down the course of the stream. She was clad in a brown leather jerkin over a long-sleeved orange blouse of light fabric. Her breeches were tan, as were the high-topped riding boots she wore. Her slender fingers caressed her chin.

"Why do we tarry here?" demanded Erimenes peevishly from his jug. The satchel that held his jar was slung from the saddle of a tall, supple-limbed riding dog, which stood lapping from the stream. Moriana had hidden the nervous gray beast on the fringe of the woods when she'd gone after the courier the night before. "I find little of interest in this stream—unless you plan to disrobe and bathe your lovely limbs, of course."

Moriana ignored him, frowning. For the third time, her lips formed the scrying spell. Once more the waters turned to milk, bubbling, frothing, swirling in meaningless patterns.

"Istu!" she cursed. The water cleared as she stood. Something was blocking her vision, preventing her from looking into the Sky City. And that something could only be the magic of her sister Synalon.

The bitch grows more powerful every day, she thought somberly. *How long before she makes her bid for power? While our mother lives, she dares little.*

*But Derora is old, and not even we of the Etuul blood
are immortal. If only my powers were stronger!*

But Moriana knew that wishing for the Sky City to
augment her magical powers was futile. She needed the
forces imprisoned in the solid bedrock of the city to per-
form her more complicated spells. And even then, her
powers were not those of her sister. And they never
would be, for she refused to make the dark pacts required to attain such magical stature.

Anxious to feel the power surging through her again,
she hurried to the top of a knoll overlooking the pool.

"Ah, how can one so beautiful be in such a foul mood
on this fine morn?" Erimenes called after her. "I'm
much in your debt, you know. Your nocturnal sporting
filled me with fresh experiences to savor. The glibness
of your lies was most illuminating."

Fost. She thought of the big man's touch, gentle with
the gentleness of great power held in check. He was no
ignorant swineherd, never. It had hurt her in the soft
dawnlight to steal from him his hope of immortality,
just as it hurt her that she'd never see him again. He
was a big man in more ways than one, hurling himself
at life with boundless energy. She could even love such
a man, perhaps.

*Maybe when the fight is done, and I hold the throne
of the Sky City.*

No, best not to think of that. There was no knowing
whether she'd survive her confrontation with Synalon.
Or whether she'd want to. If she failed, she'd certainly
be given over to her cousin, Prince Rann. The thought
made her shiver despite the growing heat. Not even the
spies she had so carefully insinuated into the ranks
of Rann's most trusted men could save her.

She brushed her hair back and gazed out over the
land. To the north and west rose mountains, blue and

indistinct with distance, in which nestled the city of Thailot. East lay many-towered Brev. Between them fell the line of the Quincunx, unmarked save for stone docks for the hot-air balloons that plied between earth and city. Following its age-old random pattern, the Sky City had recently come south from Bilsinx and veered through half of a right angle over Brev, floating ponderously and inexorably toward Thailot. From there it might swerve inwards to Bilsinx again, or head northwest to Wirix near the border of the shrunken Empire. Not even the sorceresses who ruled in the city could predict its course.

Moriana looked west. Over the horizon hung a thunderhead, ominous and dark. But no mere water vapor comprised that cloud. It was stone, black stone, the ground-spurning stone of the City in the Sky.

Desperately, Moriana longed to make straight south for the Rampart Mountains and glacier-swallowed Athalau. But she dared not stay away from the city that long. She had to return and shore up her position against the wiles of her sister. She was a few breaths younger than her dark twin, and therefore heir to the throne by law. Yet legalities would matter little if Synalon could seize power and completely crush her sister's backers. If Moriana let that happen by making the long detour to the south, not even the amulet would be of much help. With the full powers of the city to draw on, both sorcerous and military, Synalon would be virtually invulnerable.

Moriana shook her head to clear it. She *had* to have the Amulet of Living Flame. Her spies had reported to her immediately when Rann had learned of its existence. Some had died rather than warn Rann and Synalon that they had spoken. She couldn't betray their memory. And with the amulet, she could conjure and not heed agonizing death spells hurled against her. Moriana smiled grimly. She knew spells not even Synalon could ward against. But time! How those spells took time to cast! The amulet would free her from worry while she cast them.

Immortality, yes, but protection against Synalon's most deadly spells and Rann's elite bird riders rested foremost in Moriana's mind. Synalon's invulnerability would crumble, and the city would be rid of a potential tyrant.

"What?" Erimenes said as she went to her mount. "You're not going to bathe your magnificent body? Do not your garments cling and chafe with sweat? Come, come, girl, think of your health. A little cool water, a little warm sunlight on your naked, luscious breasts . . ."

"Be silent or I'll stuff your pot with mud."

"That would do nothing to me," the spirit grumbled. But he was silent for a long time thereafter.

"Ouch!" shouted the black-and-purple garbed soldier, flapping his hand in the air. "Istu piss on you, imp. You've bit me!"

From the iron box that held the fire elemental came a popping sound. "You laugh at me," the soldier snarled, clutching the wrist of his singed hand. He grabbed a dripping waterskin and brandished it. "I'll teach you, hell-wight. I'll drench the filthy life from you, Dark Ones eat me if I don't!"

"Rann will eat you if you do," said one of his comrades. The words fought their way through laughter. "Fire sprites are expensive. If the dockmaster must send down another balloon to retrieve us, and the palace mages have to conjure a fresh elemental into the bargain, you'll not gain favor in the sky."

The third soldier tamed his mirth with great effort. "We'd be lucky if we weren't left for the brigands to slay," he said, and his eyes grew serious, darting this way and that in his fat, bearded face. "I hear that all new elementals brought into being are requisitioned by the Monitors. Orders of the prince himself."

"Spreading rumors, are you," said the second man, scowling fiercely. "You know the penalty for that, don't you, Flyer Tugbat?"

The fat man snapped to attention, quivering so enthusiastically that his jowls shook like bladders.

"Y-yes, corporal."

Lying among bushes on a low hilltop overlooking the dock, Erimenes chirped with glee.

"A disciplinary infraction! Mayhap the corporal will feed the fat one to the salamander, inch by inch."

"Be quiet, you," Moriana hissed, savagely swatting at the jug. "If you give me away, I'll conjure a fire sprite into your jug."

A gurgling emerged from the clay pot. Moriana doubted that being closeted with a salamander would do the ghost any permanent harm, but the prospect clearly didn't cheer him. She filed the threat away for future use and thought hard about her problem.

These comic worms were common troopers, not bird riders. No bird-riding Guardsman would have been so foolish as to try to feed green wood to the fire elemental. The sprites were capricious enough without being antagonized in such a manner. The soldier had been too lazy to search out fuel that was properly dried, and the elemental had burned him.

It would be easy enough to take them out. One silent rush, a few thrusts of her sword, and three corpses would be cooling on the ground. But that would shout her presence as clearly as if she rode to the very porticos of the palace on a golden sky-barge borne by war-birds with jeweled pinions. Her chances of entering the city unnoticed were sufficiently slim already. She knew a better way.

The corporal finished chewing out fat Tugbat. The hapless first soldier had poured water on his injured hand and was waving it around again.

"Behold!" Tugbat roared. "Risrinc thinks he's become a war-eagle. Flap your wings, O mighty one. Fly up to your aerie."

Risrinc opened his mouth to reply. His jaw dropped farther than he'd planned. "Look," he said, pointing past his fellows.

Moriana had slid down the rear of the hill, slung the satchel over her shoulder, and boldly walked around the flank of the rise.

"Dark Ones suck my soul," the corporal said, turning. "This is a welcome sight, indeed."

"We've earned the favor of the Dark Ones," Risrinc said, his scorched hand forgotten. He leered as he said, "Look at the fine gift they've sent up."

Moriana felt fury boil in her veins. She stood before the men, legs parted slightly, head held high. "Take me at once to the Sky City," she demanded.

The soldiers exchanged glances. "Who do you think you are?" the corporal asked with a sneer. "To order the troops of the Sky City about like serfs is risky business, wench. And His Excellency Prince Rann has himself decreed that none shall be permitted to ascend without a special pass." He eyed her with his head tipped to one side and lust plain in his eyes. Her garb was outlandish, and her build taller than was common among those from the Sky City. He obviously mistook her for some slut from the Quincunx cities.

"You need a lesson in manners," he said, starting toward her. "You'll not go to the Sky City this day. Instead, you'll go with me beyond yon wall and relieve the tedium of my watch. After that, I'll let my men amuse themselves as well. Please us and we may not cut out your tongue for impertinence."

Moriana let him draw near, then casually dropped her right hand so that her fingertips touched the hilt of her sword.

"It's you who needs a lesson in manners," she raged. "Curs! On your knees before the Princess Moriana, daughter of Queen Derora, scion of the House of Etuul, Mistress of the Clouds!" Fury blazed from her like a hard, clear light.

The soldiers dropped to their knees. "Your pardon, Sky-born," gasped the corporal, rubbing his face in the black loam at her feet. "We did not know!"

"Had you knowingly addressed a princess of the Blood as you did me, you'd find yourself flayed and bathed in brine before the sun touched the Thails." She walked to the crumbling wall of the dock. The hissing roar of the fire elemental was the only sound disturbing the sudden silence. "Now," she continued, "do as you were commanded. Take me to the city at once."

The corporal struggled to his feet. He kept his eyes averted. Color seeped up from the collar of his jerkin.

"Speak, man! Why do you not obey me?"

The corporal looked at his men. They looked elsewhere. "Uh, Your Ascendancy, we . . . our orders are very strict. None is permitted up without a warrant signed by Prince Rann himself."

"Surely you don't think such prohibitions apply to me?"

"The orders were, uh, quite specific. No exceptions." He looked up at her with doleful eyes. "Please, Lady, have mercy. We are poor men who do our duty and have no wish to be exiled."

Moriana held in a sigh. She'd hoped to deal with the soldiers individually, or at least with two first, and then the other. But there was no choice now. It had to be all three at once. She hoped her absence from the city hadn't made her powers wane too much. But the nearness of the Sky City aided her. She reached out and felt the immense power flowing from the bedrock of her sky home. The magical powers mounted, then flowed smoothly, her will directing them easily.

Her eyes became disks of green fire. With a choking gasp, the corporal reeled back. The eyes became green moons, became suns, became glowing infinities engulfing the soldiers' souls.

Feeling magic near, the elemental vented a whistling scream. Moriana fought to keep her concentration. She had the two soldiers, but the corporal fought back more strongly than she would have thought possible. He didn't lightly surrender his soul.

The green, flaming eyes focused on him. His mouth worked spastically. Drool rolled down his chin. He raised trembling hands as if pleading, then jerked violently and let his arms fall limply to his sides.

Sobbing with exertion, Moriana slumped against the wind- and rain-worn wall. The three soldiers looked at her with dead eyes. The compulsion would last an hour, enough time for the corporal to ferry her to the city that loomed like a dark, oblong moon overhead, then return to his fellows and awaken, like them, with no knowledge of the encounter.

"What's this?" a querulous voice demanded. She jumped. "Have you enchanted them? Foully done! You could have slain them easily." The spirit's voice turned sulky. "You're no better than Fost. Fine behavior for a princess, if you are actually a princess."

"I am." Moriana frowned. She had no time to waste on the garrulous spirit. She turned to the corporal. "Can you hear me?"

"Yes," the man said in a distant voice.

"Good. Take me to the city, then come back here and forget you saw me. You others will forget all that has happened, also."

"As you say, Sky-born."

The wicker gondola bobbed as she climbed in. She felt a momentary surge of indignation. It seemed disgraceful that a princess must ride in such a plebeian manner. Moving stiffly, the corporal loosed the ratchet that held the great, rusted windlass immobile, dragged himself into the gondola and finally moved a ceramic lever that opened vents in the top and bottom of the fire elemental's vessel.

Air rushed in through the bottom and, heated by the sprite, billowed upwards. The red-and-white striped gasbag swelled to gravid tautness. The elemental was contained by symbols etched around the vents. Moriana could feel its fury at being confined. The rage sang along her nerve endings, as discomforting as the heat that washed from the glowing firebox.

Pulleys squealed as the balloon lifted. The ground fell away beneath Moriana's feet. Guy lines of woven silk ran from the windlass at the dock below to one set in the rock of the city. As each ground station was passed, an eagle-riding engineer flew to the next to affix guidelines for the balloons.

Moriana glanced at the corporal. He stood as rigid as death beside her; with no volition of his own, he was incapable of movement except in obedience to her commands. The woman felt triumph at having wrapped three men at once in the soul-numbing compulsion. Granted, that they were Sky City men had simplified the task. Sorcery always worked best against those already touched by magic. Sky Citizens lived intimately with enchantment, from the simple running-trim spells that kept the vast raft of skystone that was the city stable, to the powerful wards that bound Istu, dread demon of the Dark Ones.

One not so imbued with magic would prove more difficult to subdue. She doubted that all her strength and skill would have served to make Fost submissive. The courier's life-force, his will, would extinguish itself into death before permitting another mastery over his soul.

Moriana shook off the image of Fost, wondering that he'd come into her mind again. She looked about her and forgot all but the view. The Sundered Realm spread itself beneath her. Forests and mountains, plains and the distant glimmer of the Gulf of Veluz, her gaze encompassed all. Far off to the north brooded Mount Omizantrim, marked by a horizon-hugging smear of smoke from its crater.

"Poor ground-crawlers," she sighed as the wind whipped through her hair. "They know nothing of beauty, who have not seen this spectacle." The corporal did not respond.

Above, the city grew until it filled the sky.

"Is this the fabled Sky City?" asked Erimenes. His voice was muffled by the heavy, tattered cloak Moriana had wrapped about her to conceal the outland garb. "I expected somewhat more. Where are the streets paved with gold, the statues of nude maidens with perfumed wine fountaining from their nipples?"

In the crush of bodies that packed the approaches to the Circle of the Skywell, no one noticed that the voice had no attendant body.

"You're thinking of High Medurim," Moriana whispered.

"Even so, I find this tedious. Why not betake yourself to the bird rider's barracks? A woman as lusty as I perceive you to be should have her appetite no more than whetted by that mongrel Fost. But eighty, say, or ninety hot-blooded stalwarts would . . ."

She thumped the hidden jug with the butt of her hand. She'd hidden her glorious, distinctive hair in a kerchief as ragged as the cloak. She'd taken both from

a drink-sotted derelict lying stupefied by a warehouse
in the wharf district. Her new garments reeked, but
they kept the mob from pressing her too closely.

No sooner had she set foot on the ornately carved
pier jutting from the rim of the city than she had seen
a great fluttering in the sky above the city's center.
Something of importance was occurring. Chilled by
premonition, she hurried inwards along narrow streets
flanked by soaring buildings.

The human torrent carried her out into the open-
ness surrounding the Well of Winds. Moriana gasped as
she saw the procession approaching down the Skullway.

From the Palace of the Clouds the parade stretched
down the skull-paved avenue that ran broad and
straight to the Well. First came captives dressed in
greasy prison smocks, moaning and raising bound hands
in supplication. Dog riders herded them, hitting out with
clubs and jabbing with lances. Next came the band,
three hundred strong, lifting a dirge with flute, trumpet,
and somber drum. Mages followed, shaven-headed,
chanting and swinging fuming censers.

A sky-barge came after. Twelve feet square, an airy,
arabesqued framework of silver, it floated inches above
the foot-burnished skulls. Chains at its corners hung
from the harnesses of war-eagles, their great wings beating in time to the slow roll of the drums. On the barge
was spread a cushion, and on it lay an urn of dark jade.
A few steps behind, servants carried a smaller silver
litter that bore a golden vessel the size of a cooking
kettle.

Above all flew the Guards. Sunlight broke from pol-
ished helmets and the heads of lances couched in
holsters of serpent hide. At the fore flew an eagle black
as any raven. A blazing red crest adorned its head.
Moriana's heart lurched. There was no mistaking the

war mount of her cousin Prince Rann, commander of the bird riders.

Tightness gripped her throat. Her eyes stung. She tugged at the sleeve of a stout woman nearby, who was raising her voice to join the lament that wailed from the throng.

"What's happening?" she asked, pitching her voice shrill both to carry and disguise it.

The round face turned toward her was flushed and tear-bright. "You don't know?" the woman cried. "Our gracious Queen Derora is dead. She died in her sleep a night ago."

Erimenes spoke from his jug. Moriana didn't hear him. She swayed dizzily, fighting against panic, against sudden wild grief.

"By rights, Moriana should ascend the throne, and blessed would we be if that could happen. But rumor says she came to misfortune in the wastelands of the south, and I fear . . ."

A mighty shout drowned out her words. As one, the flock of bird riders descended, Ryan bringing his mount to rest on the very lip of the Well. Heads turned toward the Palace of the Clouds. Silence blossomed.

Vast black wings reached across the front of the Palace. A splendid war-bird with feathers like midnight flapped slowly along the Skullway. Hatred burned within Moriana. Here was Nightwind, greatest of all eagles, and the slim feather-cloaked figure on his back was Moriana's sister Synalon.

Moriana's fingers crushed against her palms. It was all she could do not to begin muttering a deathspell. Her sister would sense it before it was half uttered, and a swarm of Guardsmen would fall on her like owls on a mouse. Never had she felt her weakness more. If only she had the amulet now! She could conjure the spells and give Synalon the Hell Call. But the Amulet of Living Flame rested far to the south, locked in the bowels of a glacier. She had to bide her time, as much as she loathed the idea. She was still too weak and Synalon too strong.

Nightwind touched down at the head of the procession. Scarred, handsome features obscured by a sallet, Rann himself helped Synalon to the pavement. Raising her arms like wings, Synalon chanted toward the sun. Rann gestured to the dog riders.

Shouting, they drove their mounts among the captives. Driven by spear, bludgeon, and knout, the prisoners fell forward. They shrieked as they pitched into the Well. They screamed as they fell, fivescore men and women, until the prairie a thousand feet below cut short their cries.

"A sacrifice of a hundred souls!" crowed Erimenes. "This is more like it."

Tears gushed from Moriana's eyes. "Be quiet, you," she shouted at the spirit. "Be silent or I'll cast you after them!" In the uproar surrounding them, no one noted her outburst.

Singing, Synalon paced to the hovering barge, carried the jade urn to the Well, uncapped it and hurled forth its contents. She returned to the barge. Next she lifted the golden vessel. Forty feet from the Well the skull pavement ended, to reveal the marble beneath. The stately black-haired princess paced solemnly to the end of the ghastly cobblestones, set down the vessel and dropped to her knees to open it. Whiteness gleaned within.

Thus did Derora V, called the Wise, find rest after a long rule, with her bleached skull set among those of her forebears and the ashes of her remains scattered to the winds.

* * *

"No, gentlemen," said Moriana as she emerged from the passageway. "Don't rise on my behalf. I have small standing in the city these days."

The man at the head of a long, knife-scarred table shot to his feet, his face the color of the white halo of whiskers that fringed it. The others stayed seated, gaping at the golden-haired apparition who had invaded their den through a panel in what they'd believed a solid wall. A hint of wood smoke hung in the air and through closed doors drifted the sounds of thriving trade being done in the common room of the inn. Dusty sunlight fell in through cracked and fly-specked skylights, providing the room's sole illumination.

The normal crimson hue returned to the standing man's features.

"But how did you find us?" he asked. Moriana regarded him levelly. "My lady," he added, after a short pause.

Moriana's lips twisted into a smile of confidence she didn't feel. "Properly, it's 'Your Majesty,' " she said, "but I'm in no position to insist, am I? Do be seated, Councillor. Your secret's safe with me."

Uriath of the Council of Advisors to the Throne lowered himself heavily into his chair.

"I would still like to know how you found our meeting place, my lady."

She laughed. "What sort of fool do you take me for? I've long known what would follow my mother's passing. My sister is not the only one who has spies throughout the city." At a great cost in lives and effort, her agents had infiltrated Rann's intelligence network. She had known of the amulet hours before Rann and Synalon, even if she hadn't been able to prevent that knowledge from reaching them. Her thoughts turned to Kralfi, ancient but erect of stature, the palace chamber-

lain and master of Moriana's own intelligence network.
She hoped he'd made his own position secure against
Derora's death. He was more to her than a trusted
servant; he was a friend she'd loved since childhood.

"Don't worry," she continued, pulling a chair to the
head of the table and seating herself next to Uriath.
"Rann's creatures don't know of this rendezvous of
yours, or you'd be writhing on a grill this very minute."
Uriath's face lost color again.

Moriana gazed intently at the man to her right, until
he passed her a jack of ale. She'd had a long, thirsty
day. She drank deeply of the bitter brew.

Synalon obviously did not know that Uriath was head
of an underground movement dedicated to preventing
her accession to the throne. But she'd be watching him,
all the same. He had long been the voice of the loyal
opposition in council, standing against Derora in stormy
confrontations that often skirted treason. He was too
powerful to do away with out of hand, but Synalon
would watch him as keenly as any war-bird, waiting the
slip that would give grounds for his arrest.

Moriana was proud that her own spies knew more, in
this matter at least, than Synalon's. Kralfi, wise as he
was, could not easily outmatch Prince Rann's cunning.
Yet he had found out about the meeting in the back
room of the Inn of the Boiled Eel, and the hidden passage that gave access to it. One question he had not
answered. Uriath opposed Synalon. But would he back
Moriana? It was that which she had come to learn.

Another question burned more urgently within the
princess. "My mother," she asked, leaning forward.
"How did she die?"

The men eyed each other uncomfortably. "She'd not
been well for some time, Princess," a man halfway down
the table said in a high-pitched voice. "Skilled chirurgeons attended her but could not restore her

strength." He dropped his eyes uneasily from Moriana's. "She died night before last. And yesterday she was cremated and her skull purified to take its place upon the Skullway."

"The Sky City disposed of its queen with unseemly haste. Why wasn't the weeklong vigil before cremation observed, Master Tromyn?"

Tromyn bit his lip. "The mages of the Palace feared contagion."

"Do you believe that?" she flared at him. "My mother was murdered, and her body was burned to conceal evidence of the crime. Isn't that true?"

"We don't know that for a fact, my lady," Uriath said. "But it seems likely." He tipped his head to one side. "Still, what is there to do about it?"

"What I propose to do about it is claim the throne, as is my right, and bring retribution to the murderers." Moriana stared at the fleshy man in his rich, feathered robes, her eyes bright as though about to take fire in the compulsion spell. "Do you back me, Lord Uriath?"

Silence drew taut between them. To the sides, men shifted and murmured uncomfortably. Moriana held the Councillor with her gaze.

Air gusted from him. "Yes, Lady," he said. "We will."

"Master," the sooty-faced apprentice cried. "Master, look at this."

A half-smile curving his lips, Prince Rann moved to the boy's elbow. "What do you see, Inkulri?" he asked. His voice was silken.

The youth shivered. The palace mages could be arbitrary, even cruel, but next to the prince they were mild children. Inkulri was scared to the bone at having to work under Rann's direct supervision.

Now eagerness overcame apprehension. "Look,

Master," he said again, pointing to the fire-filled crystal dome. "Is that . . . isn't that the Princess Moriana?"

Rann's eyebrows rose. He leaned forward, a small, wiry man dressed in close-fitting clothes of black. His thin, hard face would have been handsome but for the network of tiny white scars that filigreed it from brow to chin.

For a moment, all he saw was the yellow dance of flame. Slowly, his skilled, pale eyes resolved the fires into an image.

"Even so, Inkulri, even so," he murmured softly. He laid a hand on the apprentice's shoulder. "You've done your city great service. It shall not go unrewarded."

He took the hand away. Inkulri shivered again, violently, despite the heat of the fire elemental trapped scant inches from his face. Somehow Prince Rann's promise of reward was more ominous than the direst threats of a master sorceror.

The warm, spicy smell of broth filled Moriana's nostrils. Gratefully, she sipped the liquid. Its heat suffused her limbs, easing her weariness. She'd had nothing to eat since—had it been just that morning?—sharing the gruel from Fost's ever-filled bowl.

Her host and hostess sat across the parlor from her. They stared at the princess as though she'd just materialized in a billow of smoke instead of being guided through a labyrinth of alleys to their house by a youthful member of Uriath's underground. They were simple, solid folk, a master stone mason and his wife, and were utterly overwhelmed by the presence of royalty.

"It's good of you to shelter me like this, Freeman Onn," she said, trying to put the man at ease. "I hope you and your wife understand the risk involved."

Onn nodded gravely. His face was as red as Uriath's,

and his hair as white. But his cheeks were rounder and he had no beard, only snowy sideburns that wisped outward an improbable distance from the sides of his face.

"No one's safe if Synalon rules," he said. "We're glad to help." His wife Ruda nodded. She was a more or less faithful replica of her husband, though without the sideburns and not balding.

Outside, the sun fell toward the forward edge of the city. The pot of broth bubbled over the hearthfire. The aroma of dove boiled with fennel and spice-lichen lent the air a homelike, comforting aroma.

His jug in its satchel propped against a wall, Erimenes sulked. Moriana had threatened him with dire punishments if he broke silence, first at the gathering of conspirators and now in the mason's house. She had enough sorcerous power to cow him, at least for the time.

A peremptory rapping on the door made Moriana start. Shaking her head, she realized she'd dozed off. The day had taken a greater toll of her endurance than she'd thought.

The knock came again. "All right, all right," Onn said peevishly. He padded to the door.

Moriana heard the door open. Onn gave a startled cry that ended in a groan. Cup poised halfway to lips, the woman looked toward the door. The black iron head of a barbed javelin jutted from the center of the mason's back.

Onn folded, leaking blood. A man in the uniform of a Guardsman stood above him, trying to pull the javelin loose. He'd used a short, heavy dart as a thrusting spear, and the barb had caught on his victim's ribs.

Ruda said nothing. She rose and went to the hearth, seemingly calm. Moriana stared from the grisly scene in the doorway to her, too stunned to move. Ruda wrapped a cloth about her hand, hoisted the pot off its rack and hurled the boiling contents into the face of her husband's murderer.

The man shrieked and fell to his knees, clawing at his scalded face. Cursing, a comrade thrust past him. Ruda stood her ground, offering no protest or resistance as he jammed his javelin into her belly, once, twice, three times, forcing her back to stain the wall of her home with blood. He grunted each time his spear point sank in flesh.

Moriana had recovered from her shock. The javelin-butt came back for another jab. A single whistling slash of her sword cut through the back of the man's neck. He twitched, evacuated his bowels and fell. Ruda dropped atop him. She died without uttering another sound.

The burned man was keening horribly. An officer barked orders as more soldiers crowded past the injured one. Moriana's sword flickered restlessly before her, scattering shards of reflected firelight.

Uriath? Had he betrayed her? If so, he'd also betrayed his own secret meeting place and the rest of the underground, as well. Not him, not from what she knew of him. But how? No time to wonder. Five soldiers faced her, poised for the attack.

"Take her alive or you'll go to Rann in her place," the officer bawled from the doorway.

The Guards closed in. They were at a disadvantage, and knew it. They'd have to grapple with Moriana to capture her, and the straight sword made that risky.

Moriana moved first. A bird rider sank with a gurgling cry, strangling on his own blood, his throat pierced. A Guard seized the woman. She raked nails across his face and kneed his groin, spun to slice open another's belly and danced back from their clutching hands.

She panted, trying to catch her wind. The officer shouted into the street. The man with the burned face lay at his feet, head hacked apart. The officer had cut him down to clear the door.

More soldiers poured in. Shouting with hopeless anger, Moriana threw herself among them, cutting wildly. Her sword bit flesh, spattering the once-neat parlor with blood.

A Guardsman ran in with a saddle-cloth taken from his war-bird outside. Moriana lunged at him. Her sword point pierced the cloth and the soldier's heart. The cloth came down over her head, blinding her.

"Marvelous! What action!" she heard Erimenes applaud. Then the soldiers bore her down.

CHAPTER
FIVE

Scarcely breathing, Fost lay on the hilltop. His cheek itched abominably. He was allergic to the oilbush, but he found no other cover on the rise overlooking the lonely balloon dock with its slumped stone walls.

A hundred yards away he'd come upon a large, long-legged dog asleep in the shadow of a cutback along a stream. Nearby lay saddle and tack of exquisite manufacture. The creature rose to its feet, surprise and sadness in its eyes, as Raissa and Wigma ran barking to sniff the riding gear. The leather was obviously ripe with the scent of gruel they'd been tracking since morning. Mount and equipage were Moriana's.

It had long been clear to Fost that the thief was making for the Sky City. Now, with the city like a stone cloud above, he would proceed afoot, as Moriana had, and see if he couldn't find a way of following her aloft.

He never doubted that she'd found a way up. When he'd peered over the top of the knoll, his guess was confirmed.

For ten minutes he'd watched the dock. The three soldiers on duty seemed occupied by some debate. He heard snatches of it—"Must have been a dream . . ." and "A sending of the Dark Ones, I tell you!" and "No, no, some joker laced our rations with dream-powder. . . ."—but paid scant attention. He was too occupied trying to form a plan.

He knew he could slaughter the three. Like most Sky City dwellers, they were short, though one was much rounder than the whip-lean norm. That lulled him little, since he'd had ample grief at the hands of small, wiry bird riders. But, by their slouching and carelessness, he guessed these three were no elite Guards. As caught up in their argument as they were, he felt sure he could sneak to within a sword's stroke of them unseen.

The problem was the balloon. He knew the principle: the fire elemental heated air, which became lighter and rose, carrying the balloon up with it along the guidelines. However, the courier had no idea how the elemental was controlled. If it was by spell, he was in trouble. He didn't relish the thought of inadvertently setting the salamander loose.

Time pressed. Its motion all but imperceptible, the Sky City passed ponderously overhead. Fost guessed that before long the sentries would have to ascend or be left behind. He had almost decided to overrun the soldiers and try to catch one alive to operate the damned balloon when something came whizzing down from the city to bounce with a *clank!* against the rusted windlass.

The soldiers jumped at the noise. They clustered around the object, a small cylinder attached to a set of pulley wheels to ride the lines. The one with corporal's insignia opened it and pulled out a message.

His face showed consternation. "I'm ordered back to the Sky City at once," he said. "I wonder what this can mean."

The others exchanged looks that said they doubted it meant well.

"This reeks of trouble," the corporal said. "If the powers above have dreamed up some imaginary misdeed to take me to task for, as the Dark Ones are my witness I'll have one of you slugs along to stick with the blame!" He gazed narrowly from one horrified trooper to the other. "You're elected, Tugbat. Haul your

round, red arse into the gondola and make ready to
lift. You'll stay, Risrinc. Give my love to the brigands."

Horror-struck, Tugbat waddled over and climbed
into the wicker basket. The corporal got in next. When
Moriana had compelled him to take her to the city, he'd
released the windlass, which meant the gasbag had to
raise the weight of the guidelines as well as the pas-
sengers. Tugbat was more knowledgeable. The gondola
was tethered to a runner on the line; the fat man undid
the clutch that made the runner grip the guy so that
the pulley inside could freewheel up the strand. The
windlass was meant to crank the balloon down.

Fost neither knew this nor cared. He saw his chance
to reach the city, if he could act fast enough.

Sword out, he was up and running down the hill even
as the elemental began to roar and the balloon began to
lift. Risrinc stood gazing up at his comrades. The sound
of a heavy footfall brought him around. Fost cut him
down. He couldn't have the young soldier seizing his
legs as he tried to climb into the gondola.

A leap, a grab, a quick heave of powerful shoulders,
and he was in the basket. His antics made it swing
wildly. Tugbat pitched against him as the corporal
shouted contradictory orders.

Fost grappled with the pudgy soldier. Tugbat was far
from his match in strength, but between the soldier's
girth and Fost's size, the three were packed snugly into
the tiny gondola. Fost had no room to maneuver. Air
blasted upward through the firebox. In panic, the
corporal had thrown the vents wide.

The balloon shot skyward. Accidentally, Fost glanced
over the side to see the ground receding at a horrible
rate. His stomach did a somersault. Ust and Gormanka
had never intended their children to be so far from earth
without solid rock of mountain or rampart beneath their
feet.

Pain seared his side. He gasped. Tugbat had drawn a dirk and was busily trying to saw him in two at the waist.

"All right, damn you," Fost bellowed. "If you're going to do that, get out and walk!" He raised the squirming trooper above his head and cast him over the side. Tugbat howled down the several hundred feet that already separated balloon from ground.

Fost had no time to watch. He turned to face a shining arc of steel. With Tugbat gone, the corporal had found space to draw his blade.

For a moment they stood, gazes locked. The corporal swayed easily to allow for the rocking of the gondola. He might be a fool, but he was more at home in this devilish contraption than was Fost. If Fost tried to draw steel he'd lose an arm. Either staying put or leaping for his foe would get him gutted, and he had no wish to follow Tugbat. That left but one way.

The corporal lunged. Breathing a prayer to his patrons, Fost sprang up and back. His hands caught shrouds, and his feet found purchase on the rim of the basket. The corporal slashed. Fost pulled up his feet. The scimitar whooshed beneath him, severing lines.

Before his opponent could ready another swing, Fost clambered up onto the rope network containing the gasbag itself. For a moment he clung like a suckling child to the giant teat that was the balloon. A jiggling in the lines told him his foe was climbing after him.

He ripped out his sword and waved it in the corporal's face. With a squeal of anger and fear, the man dropped back into the gondola. Fost shut his eyes as the balloon lurched crazily.

The taut fabric of the bag stung his cheek with heat. Curses assailed him from below. He peered down at his adversary, taking care not to let his gaze slip over the side of the gondola. The basket hung at a slight but discernible angle. The cut shroud lines had let one side drop a few inches.

Gripping the gondola's rim, the corporal began to throw his weight from side to side in an attempt to dislodge the courier. Fost gulped and clung tighter. He got a grip in the lines by his waist, timed the pitch of the balloon and bent down in a fast swoop.

The corporal dropped to the bottom of the basket as Fost's sword swung past his head. The stroke wasn't aimed at him. Stays parted with a whisper, causing the basket to tilt further. Fost reeled himself in and pressed against the flank of the balloon.

As the corporal picked himself up, Fost began to edge around the curve of the bag, his booted toes scrabbling for holds in the netting. *If everlasting life is to be filled with adventures of this sort,* he thought, *perhaps I should settle for the usual span.*

Fost ground his teeth as a blade bit into his calf. The corporal had grabbed an intact line and jumped up to slash at him. Steel ripped at Fost's legs again. He didn't try to evade the blows. If he dodged them he'd lose his grip. All he could do was hang on and hope the corporal didn't hamstring him.

Between cuts he swung down and chopped another pair of shrouds. Upright again, he chanced a look up. The Sky City loomed scant yards above the balloon. Its under-surface shone mirror-smooth and bright, and slightly convex. The stone piers of the skydock jutted like mandibles from its leading edge.

Fost leaned down and cut the final shrouds.

Balloon and gondola went separate ways. Fost had a last glimpse of the corporal's pale, astonished face. Then the basket screamed away down the guys, and the gasbag, freed from most of its load, rocketed up past the rim of the city.

At once Fost was faced with a new difficulty: the

ludicrous chance that he'd miss the Sky City altogether. Freed of the gondola, corporal, firebox, and guiding lines, the balloon rose rapidly, a breeze carrying it over the city proper. Fost wondered how long it would take the heated air in the bag to begin to cool enough for descent. He didn't have long to wait. When it came down to twenty feet above the street, he jumped clear.

Having had some experience leaping out second-story windows a pace or two ahead of sword-swinging husbands, Fost knew how to curl up and roll as he landed. Still, the impact jarred him. He measured his length on the uneven pavement, feeling as if his bones had been jolted loose from their joints.

The balloon soared again, this time freed of all burden. With a squawk and sudden boom of wings, what seemed a thousand ravens boiled from rookeries under the eaves of the high, narrow buildings all around. Cawing raucously, they circled the balloon, tearing at the gaily colored fabric. In seconds the gasbag was shredded, bits of cloth fluttering down like crippled butterflies.

Fost picked himself up, rubbing the back of his head and wondering if the knock on the skull had made him imagine the slashing attack of the ravens. But no, he saw them settling back into their nesting places, croaking in satisfaction as if they'd just repelled a major invasion.

"Ust," he moaned, "Gormanka, and the Five Holy Ones, as well."

"Those names have no power here," a voice said from behind.

He wheeled, clutching for his sword. Too late he realized he'd dropped it as he jumped. It lay on the stone, far out of reach. Then he looked at the speaker and knew he'd have no need for the weapon.

"You chose a hazardous mode of entering our city,"

she said. "The ravens attack anything that flies above
the level of the guard wall, and their talons are poisoned. Who are you, and why do you come here?"

Fost took his time answering. She was young, hardly
more than a girl, and slight with a lithe slenderness that
gave the illusion of more height. Her short-sleeved
green tunic and brief trews left her tanned, shapely limbs
mostly bare. Her face was oval, the nose fine, cheeks
softly contoured with all framed by square-cut brown
hair. Dominating the face were the eyes, as huge and
golden as coins.

"I'm Fost Longstrider, and I seek a thief."

Lips and eyes smiled as she said, "There are many
here."

"This one's name is Moriana." He bent to recover
his blade.

The girl's eyebrows rose fractionally and her mouth
tensed. From somewhere came shouts and the sound of
hobnails striking cobblestones.

"Come," she said. "The Monitors will be here soon to
see what provoked the ravens." She spun and tried to
dart into a nearby alley.

Fost caught her waist. "Where are you taking me?"

"None is allowed up from the surface since the death
of Queen Derora," she said. "Yet you rode up by balloon—alone. Did you kill the soldiers on guard below?"

"Two of them—at least." Fost grinned wolfishly.
"I'm not sure how the corporal fared."

"Then I take you to friends."

"Go, my children," Synalon purred. "Go forth and
burn the traitors out!" Blinding coruscations of yellow flame capered above the buildings. Indigo smoke,
rank with herbs and incense, roiled forth to spiral
around the sorceress.

Chittering sounds came from the three salamanders.

Their sinuous reptilian shapes flickered this way and that. Synalon clapped her hands three times and gestured at the high-arched window standing open to the dusk. Like three small comets, the elementals leaped from the grill and streaked away.

Synalon strode to the window. Three lines of light arced high and fell upon a spired building several hundred yards away. A white flash made her blink. When her eyes cleared of the pulsing afterimage, she beheld flame beginning to gleam from windows, like a hundred baleful red eyes opening.

"Spectacularly done, O Queen in all but name, but perhaps not too wisely."

Synalon whirled, her brows arching with fury. Unheard, Prince Rann had entered the room behind her. His spare frame was wrapped in a purple robe trimmed with black fur.

"As softly as you tread, still you might overstep," the princess said, her voice like poisoned honey. "Why do you think this wrong, cousin mine?"

Rann went to the window. Already flames reached high from the doomed building. The fire's rushing bellow mingled with the screams of the inhabitants.

"Such displays serve only to incite the populace. There are better ways to deal with dissent."

"Calamanroth dared speak openly against me. Thus do I demonstrate my power, and the fate awaiting those who do not acknowledge my supremacy." She gazed narrowly down on him. "I'd think you'd find this most diverting."

The prince smiled. "Wholesale destruction interests me but little. My pleasures are more intimate." He gazed from the window. Outside it was as if the sun rose in the north. Over the crackle of the flames an eerie wailing soared: the triumphant ululation of the salamanders. "The fire sprites are fickle beasts, mindless and cruel. Have a care they don't get out of hand."

"I can control them!"

"One hopes so." The smile never wavered on Rann's lips. This game was not as risky as it seemed. Even in her most frenzied rage, Synalon would not lightly toss away a tool as useful as Rann. Barred by gender from the line of succession, his ambition could never grow to threaten her. Both knew it. So, like a court fool, he could speak as he pleased without fear of retribution. And Synalon knew his sense of duty ran deep. For her, he would do anything. "Still, there are better uses for them."

"Such as?" Synalon stood back pettishly ignoring the fiery display she had created. Prince Rann's carping had spoiled the amusement for her.

"Surveillance. Given sufficient sprites, our watchers can attune to any fire lit within the confines of the city. Any business transacted by flamelight, whether of taper, hearth, or furnace, will be revealed to us."

Synalon frowned. She felt stirrings of interest at the idea, but was too piqued at her cousin to admit it.

"Is there any practical application for this folderol?"

"You may judge for yourself, Princess." From within his robe he produced a bell. "Here is a captive taken as a result of our fire scrying. Or perhaps I should say captives."

He rang the bell. The silver-bound doors of the chamber opened. A squad of bird riders entered, dragging a prisoner with them. They flung the captive forward. She fell to hands and knees with a ringing clatter of heavy chains. She shook back matted hair of gold and raised her head.

Synalon gasped as she looked upon her sister. She recovered quickly.

"How sweet of you," she said, "to come in this sad hour to console me over our dear mother's death."

"Words, words, I'm surfeited by words," a voice said peevishly. "When does the torture begin? Or barring that, the debauchery?"

Synalon's sapphire eyes widened. "What's this?" she demanded of Rann. "These words that come from thin air. Is it . . .?"

"It is." The prince bowed low. A soldier handed him a stained satchel of the kind carried by Realm-road couriers. "My lady, may I present to you Erimenes the Ethical, late of Athalau."

He opened the bag and took forth a plain earthenware pot. "My blessing on you, good sir," the spirit said. "I was sick nigh unto death of the stench of that gruel leaking all day from Kest-i-Mond's bowl."

Synalon clapped her hands with delight. "You may name your reward this night, Prince Rann," she said. "In these two you have brought me the means by which I shall restore the lost greatness of the Sky City!"

"My reward is serving you, my queen." Rann bowed deeply, his mouth curling into a slight sneer to hide other emotions, which he could never sate.

She stroked her sister's cheek. Moriana glared at her. Synalon asked, "Tell me, Rann, how was this deed done?"

"While I possess no magical powers of my own, others who do were posted to observe. Somehow, your sister made her way undetected into the city. A sprite-watcher noticed her in the household of a traitor. We sent a squad of Guardsmen to fetch her."

"Were these traitors long nurtured by her?"

"I'm sure she was brought to them by someone else whom she contacted on arrival. I fear organized resistance has sprung up already."

"No doubt the traitors have been induced to name

their cohorts." The princess returned to the window. The house of Calamanroth slumped into itself and sent livid sparks high into the nighttime sky.

Prince Rann's smile turned feral. "I fear not, my lady." Synalon spun and angrily faced him. "The fool of a captain in charge of the detachment allowed his men to slay all but Moriana. Moreover, he got five men cut up in the capture."

"I trust he has been . . . chastised."

"He is chained naked in my aerie, with his belly slit open for Terror to dine upon his entrails," Rann said. His eyes showed more animation than at any time since entering Synalon's chamber.

"You coddle that bird overmuch," Synalon said sulkily.

"Oh? And did you not feed your serving maid's eyes to your own Nightwind when you caught her pilfering your jewels?" He chuckled, a sound like coins falling into a silver cup. "It increases the mettle of a war-eagle to taste man-blood now and then."

Moriana had floated in a daze since being clubbed senseless by the bird riders. Seeing her sister and cousin had whipped away the mental fog. She sat up straight and fixed her kin with a gaze of fine contempt.

"You two have changed little since last I saw you. You're still wicked children delighting in the torment of small, helpless creatures." She spat upon the marble floor.

"Is this the courtesy you show us? We, who are your loving family?" Rann towered above her, hands on slim hips.

Moriana's lips curled. "Speak not of loving, half-man." Rann went dead white. "You knew nothing of what it meant even before the mountain people burned off your manhood."

"You said I might name my reward," Rann said to

Synalon, his face a mask of awful rage. "I name it now: give me this slut, that I might pleasure her with death lasting long days."

"You shall not have her, Rann. Choose some other token." A slim hand raised to check his outburst. "Stay. I'll not argue now. I would speak with our other guest."

Synalon sat in an ornate chair carved from a single beryl. Tormented visages looked forth, not wholly human. They seemed compounded subtly of the features of men in anguish and the serpents devouring them. At a languid gesture, a soldier placed a similarly carved stand in front of her, and another set Erimenes's jug upon it.

"Welcome to the Sky City, ancient one," Synalon greeted.

"You are Princess Synalon? You rule this city?"

Synalon's eyes flicked at her sister like a scorpion's sting. "I am Synalon, yes. As to the question of my rule, my sister would deny it, though I feel she'll repent her error soon."

"Not while I live!" shouted Moriana.

"My meaning precisely."

The golden-haired princess slumped back. The sick certainty of defeat washed over her. *My failure will cost me my life,* she thought bitterly. *But what shall it cost my city?*

"Your sister doubtless knows countless secrets regarding those who conspire against you," Erimenes said. "Why not put her to the torture to wrest the information from her?"

Synalon looked at the jug. "You surprise me, sage. As I recall, the philosophy you taught in life was utter disavowal of wordly considerations. It's not easy to reconcile that outlook with your desire to witness torture."

"Bright lady, know that on the occasion of my death I foreswore all my foolish theories of abstinence," Erimenes explained. "I glory in seeing life, raw life, be it in pleasure or in pain. Bring on the whips, the pincers, the red-hot irons! I've never watched a rousing torture."

"Shall I do as he suggests, Princess?" Rann tongued his lips in anticipation. Seeing that slight action made Moriana wince.

"No!" Synalon sliced the air with her hand. "I've other uses for her, uses requiring that her body remain unsullied by your gentle mercies."

Rann's face paled with anger again. Synalon rose to her feet, glaring down at the prince.

"Do you think I'm being arbitrary?" she demanded. "Do you think that I wouldn't like to take blade in hand and peel this bitch's hide from her cringing body? Yet that is a pleasure I will forego for a greater reward."

She strode across the chamber. A breeze stirred the heavy blue and green tapestries that decorated the walls. The murky, somber designs were highlighted by the raging fire across the city. The scent of burning made the wind bitter on Synalon's tongue.

"Long have I planned for this moment." Synalon said. "Long have I dreamed, step by careful step, of the torments with which I'd end my sister's life. I would cut her and burn her and flay the skin of her face to make a rag for menials to swab the cesspipes. And I would keep her alive, oh, so long, so very long."

She stood above Moriana. Her sister stared up at her in untrammeled horror. Smiling, she took Moriana's face gently in her hands.

"Yes, she is beautiful, almost as beautiful as I. Despoiling such beauty is a rare privilege, even for one with my power. There were times when I'd have given up my hope for the throne to behold my sister squirming as the flames gnawed on her tender flesh; such is my hate.

"So do you conceive of what it means to me to forego my vengeance, cousin?" She stood so close that the moon-pale globes of her breasts, scarcely contained by the low-cut velvet gown, touched the prince's chest. Synalon moved closer, her hand brushing quickly, teasingly, over his empty crotch. His jaw set and tawny eyes flickered. The scars shone forth in the intensity of the Prince Rann's emotion, making it appear that a fine gossamer mesh covered his face.

Synalon pirouetted away, leaving him trembling from her taunting nearness. She evoked passions in him that could not be sated. Not directly.

But captives would howl their anguish that night.

"Take my sister to the dungeon, and let no harm befall her. Otherwise you'll answer with what remains of your soul, Rann."

He clasped hands to breast and bowed.

At a signal, the Guardsmen pulled Moriana to her feet. She didn't resist as they marched her from the chamber. Her last sight before the doors slammed shut was of her sister leaning forward on her throne, in eager conversation with the spirit in the jar.

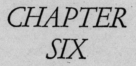

CHAPTER
SIX

"If you move the blade over a bit farther to the left you can sever the artery," Fost said, rolling his eyes down to look at the fist holding the dagger to his throat. "Is this what passes for friendship in the Sky City?"

His guide stood before him in the dusk, an enigmatic look in her eyes. "Perhaps so. All depends on your telling the truth—why do you seek the Princess Moriana?"

"Princess? She's no princess. She's a lying, thieving, yellow-haired harlot! She robbed me. I trailed her here."

The blade tightened at his throat. He felt a sting as skin parted and a trickle of blood oozed forth.

"Let me slit his throat, Luranni," a brusque young male voice growled from behind Fost's ear. "He's a foul spy. A creature of Rann's."

Luranni sucked in her breath and heaved a deep sigh. "You've said this Moriana is yellow-haired. Is she tall, well built, carrying a straight sword which she can use as well as any man?"

"By the Holy Ones, yes! She nearly spitted me with that thing last night."

"That is the princess."

I knew her tale was a lie, Fost thought. *But a princess!*

"His story's as thin as one of Synalon's gowns, Luranni," the youth who held him said. "Why would our princess rob a lowborn scum like him?"

111

"Doubtless she had her reasons," Luranni said. "What is this property you claim to have lost? Is it valuable?"

"It . . ." Fost stopped. He couldn't very well tell the flat truth. A treasure such as Erimenes held the key to would cause a saint to murder his mother. "In truth, I don't know. I'm a courier. I had a parcel to deliver. She took it. It's not my business to poke into the items I deliver, but it is my business to make sure I deliver them."

The youth with the knife made a skeptical sound. Fost wondered how his attacker would react if he knew the circumstances under which Moriana had gotten the satchel.

"Look, I know I've not shaved today, but I prefer to tend to such details myself. Kindly call off your budding barber."

Luranni laughed musically. "Erlund, release him."

"Not until we . . ." Before he'd finished, Fost ran a hand up to grip the knife hand, and jabbed his elbow back into the pit of the young man's stomach. Erlund doubled over, gagging. The big man spun out, wrenching the arm so that the knife cartwheeled away, to clink against a wall. His boot lashed out. Erlund grunted and collapsed.

"Erlund should learn to obey orders." Fost felt his neck, winced and brought away bloodied fingers.

"Think no ill of him. He's upset with himself. Just three hours ago he guided the princess to a house we thought safe from her sister's spies. Not long after, bird riders broke in, slew our folk, and captured Moriana."

Fost stared at her. He felt ill. Of all the places he might have had to penetrate to retrieve the philosopher's shade, by far the worst was the keep of the rulers of the Sky City. It was just like Erimenes. Fost kicked a wall, hurt his toe, and cursed volubly.

He sensed others approaching. "A bargain," he said quickly. "I'll help you rescue your princess, on condition that the parcel be returned to me, unopened and unharmed."

"How much help can you offer?" Luranni said skeptically. "You were led easily into our trap."

Fost's laugh made her take a step back. "Led? No, I came of my own free will, eyes open to the danger."

"Words!" spat Erlund.

"You think so? Listen: two of your friends were on our tails before we'd gotten out of sight of the docks. We acquired two more escorts as we passed the warehouse with the broken windows and the woman-breasted gargoyles. A final four drifted out of doorways in our wake as we turned onto this block."

The courier turned a malevolent grin on Erlund, who stood slightly stooped, his tow-colored hair dangling in front of eyes that blazed hate.

"Moreover," Fost continued, directing his words to Luranni, "your bright young lad's shoes scuffed cobblestones as he came for me. If I hadn't wanted to deal with you, I'd have spitted him like a fowl to be roasted for dinner."

"That's a lie!" Erlund struggled to get free of the friends who held him upright.

Luranni shook her head. "No. He's right." A vee of consternation creased her smooth brow as she regarded Fost in the waning light. "Very well, Longstrider. You have your bargain. Follow me. We go to meet my father."

The shadowed shapes of Luranni's comrades faded back into the gloom. Luranni turned to go with them. Realizing Fost was not following, she halted and turned.

"We must hurry," she said, fluttering impatient fingers.

Fost stood where he was, as dark and unmoving as a basalt statue. "I don't reject your hospitality," he explained, "but I can't help thinking of where it got Moriana."

One of the youthful conspirators rematerialized from between two buildings close at hand. "No fault of ours," he said. "That damned bitch-slut Synalon has her sorcerors mentally attuned to a horde of fire elementals. The salamanders can see anything lit by flame, and what they see, Rann and his henchmen see as well." He showed white teeth in a lupine grin. "That's one thing we gained from this disaster. Seizing the princess so quickly showed they had some special source of information; her whereabouts were known only to a select few, who would not hope to escape Rann's mercies no matter whom they betrayed."

"The city reeks of fire-magic," Luranni said. "It took little time for us to realize what our enemies were doing."

Fost's stomach iced over again. He'd known from the beginning he dealt with utter amateurs. It was no comfort to have a demonstration of how skillful his enemies were in contrast.

"You mean that so much as lighting a taper would give us away to this Rann?"

Luranni's mouth opened to reply. Blinding white light abruptly washed the storefronts on the far side of the avenue. Fost, Luranni, and several of her cadre ran into the center of the street.

To the east, the soaring Palace of the Clouds dominated the skyline. From the palace's highest tower sprang three lines of flame tipped with incandescence. Fost could feel the stinging, hungry heat beat against his face as the three points of brilliance hung for a moment like new stars in the night sky. They plunged down like meteors, leaving glowing trails. Stone melted before them and wood exploded into fire. Like water thrown up by a falling stone, red flames splashed high into the ebon sky.

"Such is the vengeance of Synalon," Luranni said at Fost's side. Her fingertips were soft and tremulous on his brawny arm. "Such is her power."

The stricken mansion vomited flame like an erupting volcano. Fost had a vision of lovely Moriana held captive by a power and malice that hurled fire elementals against those who opposed it. The thought brought an upwelling of heat within him to match the dragon's-breath that washed over his face.

Cold sobriety quenched the emotional burst. *Why waste my concern on her?* Fost thought. *She robbed me and tried to deny me eternal life.* Deep within a voice reminded him that she'd done far more than that. He ignored it and let Luranni lead him away.

The limits imposed by the city's circumference meant that space was at a premium. Streets tended toward labyrinthine narrowness. Buildings lofted high and slender, so tall they seemed to lean together at their tops to form an arcade of dizzying height. Yet here and there the elaborately graven stone walls fell away, to let a small fountain play gently in a trim garden, or a statue brood in silence. Fost came to understand this was to keep the inhabitants of the city from losing intimate contact with the sky that was their home.

As they walked, Luranni filled Fost in on recent events in the Sky City. She spoke of the long-standing enmity between the royal twins Synalon and Moriana, of the long illness and abrupt demise of Queen Derora, of Moriana's absence and disastrous return. Her voice was low music, transforming the lilting accent of the city into a liquid concerto.

"How did you come to meet our princess?" Luranni asked.

He craned his neck around, framing his response carefully. The scene was eerie enough to make his distraction convincing. A dancing interplay of shadow and orange hellglare destroyed all perspective. The distorted figures peopling the friezes that clung to the narrow facades seemed to move with a life of their own.

"We fell in with one another on the road from Samadum," he said, deciding to heed wisdom learned long ago in the slums of High Medurim. *The simplest lie serves best,* the wise old thief to whom he'd been apprenticed had said over and over. "She showed interest in a parcel I was to deliver in the Southern Steppes. Perhaps she believed it contained property stolen from her; I don't know. I do know she drugged me, and when I awoke my sled-dogs trailed her here."

"Odd that they were able to," Luranni said. "Moriana is a sorceress, as are all of noble birth in the city. I'd have thought she'd possess tricks to throw your beasts off the scent."

"I have a few tricks of my own," Fost said, smiling down at her.

A quick pressure on his arm halted him. "Here," Luranni said. "My home." She gestured to a wood-fronted building three stories tall, sandwiched between structures high enough to snag passing clouds. The fireshot darkness made it impossible to discern details, but Fost had the impression they'd passed into a more genteel district than that fronting the docks.

With a trace of a smile on her lips, she lifted a finger and signaled for silence. Taking his arm, she led him up the short flight of steps to the triple-arched door. Courteously, Fost reached a hand out to open it but found it locked. Luranni gestured and it slowly opened before them.

Inside was blacker than in the street. Fost paused in the door as the girl glided down a short hallway. He expected her to light a candle. She stopped at the foot of a dimly seen stairway and turned back expectantly. He realized there would be no candle within this house while he was there—no fire at all. All flames were Synalon's eyes within the city.

She took his hand and led him up the stairs. Behind them he heard the door swing softly shut. The hairs at the back of his neck lifted slightly. This wasn't called the City of Sorcery for nothing.

His toe slammed into a projection at the second-floor landing. Luranni smiled at his curses. He could see her face in the starlight filtering in through window slits.

She led him to a doorway masked by a bead curtain. She swept it aside and nodded for him to enter. Ducking his head, he entered the chamber. He discovered painfully that he couldn't stand upright. The ceiling was meant to clear the heads of the locals, not someone of his large stature.

The curtain fell back with a tinkle like tiny chimes. Luranni walked by Fost and plucked something off a shelf, untroubled by the darkness.

"Well," Fost said. "When does your father arrive?"

Luranni laughed. "Do you seriously think High Councillor Uriath would welcome being dragged from his dinner to speak with some ragged groundling?" Mention of dinner brought a growl from Fost's stomach. "We will see him in the morning. Sit and I'll bring food."

"I'll be forever in your debt."

He found a fat, silky cushion against a wall and lowered himself onto it. Relaxing, he began to battle drowsiness. He'd had a long and tiring day, and not much sleep the night before.

Luranni returned from another room with food and a jug of wine. She pulled up another cushion and sat facing him, the food between them. In one hand she held the object she'd taken from the shelf. She raised it and shook it briskly.

Light flooded the room. Fost froze with a morsel of spiced meat halfway to his open mouth. His blood cried *betrayal!* and his pulse hammered in his temples.

Luranni set the lamp down and clapped her hands delightedly. "Oh, but you looked so astonished when the lightfool came on!" she sang.

"You'll look more astonished when five dozen bird riders drop in through the skylight."

"There's no fire here." Luranni's eyes were alive with mirth. "Creatures so minute they cannot be seen individually reside within. When they are disturbed, their bodies give off light, but no heat." She tapped the clear glass figurine with a fingernail. Waves of greater brightness rippled through it. "They're North Cape magic, common toys here in the city." She shook her hair as she filled a bronze goblet with wine. "I never thought my little fool would prove so useful."

Chewing on a savory strip of meat, Fost leaned closer to examine the lamp. It had been blown in the shape of a jester at the court of High Medurim, hang-bellied and great-eared, naked but for a breechclout. Cool radiance pulsed from it. Far from being dazzling in its brilliance as he'd thought when its light first shone, the glow was soft and calming to his twisted nerves.

He sat back. Having taken a bite of food, he was overcome with a hunger so great that he felt a mad desire to stuff handfuls of the sweet, hot meat and little pastries into his mouth.

"Tell me of the Sky City," he said, hoping to eat his fill while she spoke.

Luranni gazed a moment into the fool's glow, sipping wine. "Very well," she said. "Your height is great, your bones massive. You are northern-born, aren't you?"

Fost nodded as he gulped down a mouthful of pastry. "I was born in the Teeming, the slum district of High Medurim itself."

Luranni was still. She rocked back and forth, long, graceful legs tucked under her, eyes gazing into the light. Just as Fost began to wonder if she were entranced, she spoke again. "Twelve thousand years ago men came to this land. Your ancestors came from the cold mountains and forests of the Northern Continent; they founded the city-states that later grew into empire. From the Islands of the Sun came my own folk, to make landfall in the southeastern corner of the continent. The Realm was sparsely inhabited. Beings lived here, manlike and yet not men; warm-blooded and shaped like us, but with the scales of reptiles. Their women nursed their young at the pap, but the young were hatched from eggs. *Zr'gsz* they called themselves, *the People*. Men named them Vridzish, the Hissing Ones, after their manner of speech. At first there was amity. The People were an ancient race and barely noticed the newcomers."

She paused and moistened her throat from the goblet. Fost found his eyes slipping from her face and moving down the graceful curve of her throat to the shadowed valley between her breasts. Her breasts were not large, but the slice of each, visible where her tunic had come loose, looked tender and inviting. With his hunger beginning to be sated, Fost felt a new appetite asserting itself. He bid his manhood be still and forced his eyes up to hers.

"High Medurim was built by the Northbloods, Athalau by the People of the Sun. Inevitably their domains spread. Cities rose in what is now the Quincunx: Wirix on its island in Lake Wir, Thailot at the head of the pass connecting the lands east of the Thail Mountains with Deepwater on the western shore. From Athalau were settled Kara-Est, at the head of the Gulf of Veluz, and Brev, which lay on the trade route between Athalau and Deepwater. Later, Medurim and Athalau joined to build Bilsinx, the central city of the Quincunx, to protect the strategic junction of routes from north to south and east to west.

"The Hissing Ones grew uneasy. They had little use for the surface, save for their skystone mines in the lava beds of Mount Omizantrim, from which they built their skyrafts and the very city itself, launched twenty thousand years before. Most were content to dwell here, depending on trade with the groundli—uh, the surface folk, for food. But they came to fear that Man would try to topple them from their city. The city was not confined to the Quincunx then, but traveled where its owners wished. Whoever controlled the city ultimately controlled the Realm. This was a balmy land in those days, and humankind is covetous. It would not long permit ownership to remain in other hands."

"Wait," Fost protested. "You said this land was balmy, and before that you said the Northern Continent was cold. Living this far south you might think that, but traders plying northward from High Medurim take only light garb with them and need extra stocks of water due to the heat. And where we sit this instant, we're not two hundred miles from the Rampart Mountains, and south of them lie ice fields. You've been sadly mislead, Luranni."

"I said this is how things *were,* outlander. Haven't you heard of the War of Powers?"

"Vaguely." Fost shrugged and drank some wine. "Mere legends, no more."

"Oh? Untrue. Listen: the sorceries of the Hissers were great, beyond even those of Athalau. The People held captive a demon, black Istu, against whom neither might nor magic could avail. They decided to cleanse the Realm of humanity. For a hundred years they systematically slaughtered, laying waste the Quincunx cities and whipping the armies of High Medurim off the battle field like curs to the kennel." Fost scowled at this description of his forebears but did not interrupt. "Their skyborne armies usually overwhelmed, but when they didn't, the Demon of the Dark Ones strode forth across the land. The earth itself groaned beneath their might.

"At last only Athalau remained unconquered. All of humankind that survived north of the Ramparts was a few thousand pitiful refugees, too weak to threaten the People. Athalar wisdom was great enough that even with Istu's aid the Hissing Ones didn't wish to go against the folk of that city until they were completely isolated. That time came at last.

"Even then, the Athalar had come to be more of the other world than of this one. One alone in that city, Felarod the Mystic, preached the call to arms against the People. The Athalar did not heed him, scorning him for his materialistic concerns. A few listened, though, and began to work secretly with him.

"In Athalau lived five prophets who had dwelt among men since long before the colonization of the Realm, and who were sacred to the Wise Ones of Agift. These five went to the Sky City to intercede for Athalau. The Hissing Folk laughed and sacrificed them to Istu, after inflicting terrible tortures."

"The Five Holy Ones," Fost said in surprise.

"Just so. The Three and Twenty Wise Ones gave their blessing to Felarod, which enabled him to open the Gate of the Earth-Spirit. The very planet had been outraged by the tread of the star-born demon; its power surged, channeled by Felarod and his hundred acolytes.

"The conflict was fierce beyond imagining. A star fell from the sky and blasted a great crater in the Southern Steppes; in the west the great island of Irbalt sank beneath the sea; the very planet tipped on its axis, bringing the Realm almost to the South Pole, and the Northern Continent into the tropics. At last the People were overcome. Nine out of ten died, as did ninety of the Hundred. As great as was the power he guided, Felarod couldn't destroy or banish Istu. He did manage to trap the demon within the foundations of the city, with wards that would last an eternity. All but dead, he summoned up the Ullapag from the guts of Mount Omizantrim to guard the skystone beds and to keep the surviving People away from this last resource of their strength. Then he gave himself back to the Earth-Spirit."

Luranni sighed. Though the evening was cool, sweat beaded her brow. "Little of the tale remains. The People sued for peace. They renounced all claim to the surface world and restricted the path of the city to the Great Quincunx. The survivors of Felarod's Hundred, appalled at the destruction they'd wreaked, exiled themselves. Later, Athalar came to dwell in the Sky City. Eventually they became strong enough to banish the People and claim the city for themselves." She sat back, drawing into herself. She had chanted the tale like a priestess reciting a litany. Now that it was done, she seemed as spent as if she'd performed some complex and demanding ritual. "Beyond that, our story is of rise to glory and eventual decline. I imagine it's as depressing to me as the story of High Medurim's fall from mastery of the Realm to nominal lordship over a handful of squabbling city-states must be to you."

Fost shrugged. The past glories of High Medurim meant nothing to him; they were too far past, and the gilded and hollow empire was now too plainly a joke. He poured himself more wine and refilled Luranni's cup. All the while, his eyes kept drifting toward the floor.

"Is it true a demon lives beneath our very feet?" he asked at last.

The girl nodded solemnly. "In earlier times, the rulers could partially awaken it and tap some of its strength, though they couldn't free it, even if they had been fools enough to try. The Rite of Dark Assumption was performed at the accession of each new ruler. It involved the sacrifices of one of the royal blood to Istu."

For a moment, Fost had trouble swallowing his wine. "Do they still do that?" The fear in him did not spring solely from self-interest.

Moriana ...

"No. Not since the Etuul dynasty came to power five thousand years ago. Derora was of that lineage, as is Moriana—and Synalon as well, though you'd hardly know it."

Vague worries still gnawed at Fost's brain. He realized Luranni was leaning forward, her tunic opened farther, her red lips parted. Her eyes turned to glowing moons.

The fears evaporated, and with them all thoughts of the thieving princess. Fost touched Luranni's cheek. She kissed the rough, scarred fingers, never taking her luminous eyes from his face. The faint, exotic aroma he'd noticed on entering the apartment thickened, became a heady musk, intoxicating and arousing. He recalled her saying that all nobles of the Sky City possessed some sorcerous power, and as a High Councillor, whatever that was, her father was undoubtedly of exalted birth. The great-eyed girl had worked some enchantment on him. The musk grew stronger, caressing his palate with a taste of cinnamon. He recalled a similar taste in the wine. Then he pushed such things from his mind; he took Luranni into his arms.

Her mouth opened. His covered it eagerly. Her tongue danced over the very tip of his. She pressed his hand to her breast. Warm flesh yielded to his touch. Her nipple throbbed its urgent need against his palm.

Their tongues flowed together. His hands, at once rough and gentle, tugged open her tunic with a *snap!* of the lacings. Her own fingers deftly undid the front of his garment, and stroked coolly across his hirsute chest.

His mouth left hers. Her lips glistened moistly in the heatless light. He nibbled down the line of her jaw. His hands kneaded the pliant softness of her breasts as he felt the lustful hammering of her pulse beneath.

His lips brushed down the curve of her throat. There was tension in the fingers that peeled Fost's tunic away, tension and need. The courier kissed the soft, pale ripeness of her left breast. A quiet, "Oh!" broke from the girl's gleaming lips.

Fost worked the succulent melon with his lips as ravenously as he'd devoured the bread and meat the woman had set before him earlier. Her scent was like the scent of the wine, strong and sweet. Her ivory teeth pinned her lower lip as she sucked in her breath in passionate response. One slim hand trapped the courier's head against her small, firm breast. The other caressed the cabled muscles of his back.

Questing fingers found a long transverse wound.

Luranni felt Fost stiffen. "You've been wounded," she murmured. She pushed him away reluctantly.

At the girl's silent urging, Fost hoisted himself into a sitting position. Naked from the waist up, Luranni went to a low table, picked up a silver jar and from it began to apply a stinging cream to the swordcut.

Gradually the fire died, and with it the last of the residual ache that had not left Fost's back since the bird rider's blade had laid it open.

"Thanks," he said, unable to keep a note of grumpiness out of his voice. "But I can think of other, better things you can do to heal me."

"You flatter me, Longstrider," she said. "But lie back down and I'll do what I can."

Fost obeyed. The cream had dried on contact with his skin. The silky covering of the pillow soothed him further. He vented a throaty sigh of contentment.

Like a vision she appeared before him. She was nude, her lithe limbs shining as though oiled. Dark aureoles covered her breast-tips like palms, and the nipples jutted proudly erect. The fur beneath her flat belly was fine and brown. In the tangled ringlets between her thighs, a drop of moisture threw back the fool's-light like the facets of a reflecting diamond.

Fost's sigh became a growl of lust. He started to lunge for her, his hand reaching outward.

"No, no," she laughed, tossing back her straight hair. "Rest. I shall do what is necessary." With strong, insistent hands she pushed him back down.

Without seeming to move quickly, she had the big man's trousers and rough undergarment off in an instant. His manhood swung upright like a flagpole. Luranni's eyes and mouth smiled in appreciation of what she'd found.

"It's truly spoken that northern men are mighty," she murmured.

She swung a slender leg across him. His hands caught her about the middle and slowly lowered her down. Rolling her hips in subtle circles, Luranni leaned forward. Fost's hands left her waist to slide up her ribs and grasp the rounded cones of her firm breasts.

She gasped at the rough pressure of his hands. She threw away all restraint and began to drive Fost wild. Time ceased to have meaning. In a vague, detached corner of his mind not blinded with a red fog of lust, Fost thought that Luranni had not lain with a man for some time. But then, he'd coupled passionately with Moriana the night before, and here he was, as ready and randy as if he'd been six weeks on the road with only his dogs for company.

Not even the thought of Moriana could quell his rampaging desire, such was Luranni's magic. Sweating, straining, groaning, they built the sweet electric tension until it burst free in loin and brain and fused their souls with ecstasy.

When the fury was done, Luranni fell forward, laughing her springtime laugh. For a long time they lay still, with murmurings and small caressings, content with the feel of each other close.

"I see a question building in your eyes," Luranni said after a while. She raised herself to look at the courier's face. In the soft glow of the fool, his features looked curiously young and vulnerable. "I haven't the power of thought-scrying, so you'll have to speak it with your lips."

She broke into giggles as he darted his head up and kissed her on the nose. He patted her upturned rump affectionately, but his face grew serious at once.

"This Rite of Dark Assumption," he said. "What did it achieve? The demon cannot be summoned or released, you said. Did the ritual serve just to do away with troublesome rivals to the throne?"

A shudder passed through her naked body. She rolled off him, clinging to his side for comfort. "No, not that. Or rather, not that alone." Her golden eyes were grave. "So great was the magic with which Felarod bound Istu that the demon cannot fully be wakened by any magic men know, though the People could perhaps achieve it—if any of them survive and still remember. But Istu's dreams are filled with power and vengeance. The rulers of the Sky City tapped into them, winning the good will of the slumbering demon with sacrifice."

She lay unspeaking for so long that Fost thought she had fallen asleep. Just as he was about to stir, she spoke again. "Even asleep and bound, Istu's strength is vast. With that power augmenting their own sorcerous knowledge, the rulers of the city challenged the empire during its most powerful epoch."

Fost nodded. He knew of the wars between High Medurim, at the peak of her glory, and the Sky City. Eventually High Medurim had triumphed, with the aid of mages he now guessed to have come from Athalau. But victory had proven costly. Driving the human Sky Citizens back into their floating stronghold hadn't required such cosmos-wrecking magic as had the defeat of the People, but it had sapped the strength of the empire enough so that in a century invading barbarians from the hot Northern Continent had seized the Sapphire Throne and started High Medurim on its own road to decay.

"So they gave up the Rites?" he asked.

"Julianna the Wise, who wrested the crown from Malva Kryn and founded the Etuul line, forbade it as an abomination. The rulers of the city would no longer rule through power gained from the anguish of sacrifice." Absently, she stroked the great muscles of his chest. "Our sorcery is still the strongest in the Realm, but not what it once was."

Her voice rang dim and far away in Fost's ears. Too much exertion and too little sleep had finally wore him down. The thought fluttered through his mind that Synalon, from what he had learned, was formidable enough without the aid of sleeping Istu. The fool's-glow began to dim. Fost slipped into deep sleep with his hand resting on Luranni's silken flank.

"Greetings, cousin." Moriana looked up from the bottomless well of her misery to see Prince Rann standing in the doorway of the torture chamber.

Like a malevolent spirit he glided across the floor, feet soundless on stone worn smooth by the feet of generations of torturers and their victims. His limbs were cloaked in a robe of dark gray silk that shimmered in the light of the bracketed torches. With his hair slicked back from his ruined, aristocratic face, he looked like an idle noble come to while away the night at some mild diversion.

Which is exactly why he comes to this room, she thought. As another might compose sonnets or contemplate ancient statuary, Rann took his rest and pleasure in the contemplation of pain. For all her physical courage, Moriana shuddered at his touch.

The examination was as thorough and impersonal as any physician's. Few chirurgeons possessed the eunuch prince's knowledge of human anatomy. None could have gained it as he had, by testing living bodies to destruction in a thousand hideous ways, without violating the powerful oaths binding them to the cause of healing.

"You are well, I judge, outside of being helpless from the ward spells Synalon cast on this cell," he said, rising. "A few bruises caused by that lout of a captain.

I daresay he's sorry. At least he seemed so when Terror ripped out his liver. Your hurts are nothing the blessed queen can lay to me."

"By what right do you call her queen?" Moriana flared. "I am the younger by seven minutes. By law I am ruler of the city!"

He smiled. "Cling to your pride, my dear. It's all you have. Soon enough even that will be torn from you." His face darkened. He was still bitter at being prevented from torturing his cousin.

He has been scrupulous in following Synalon's orders regarding her sister. Moriana's torn garments had been replaced with a clean but shapeless linen smock, prisoner's garb; the chains that bound her wrists and ankles were carefully padded with silk to prevent chafing. Synalon's instructions hadn't mentioned Moriana's mental well-being, however, so Rann had conveyed her here to what he liked to refer to as his study, where incense and scrubbings with lye had done little to mask the raw stench of death and pain.

The sound of voices made Rann turn. Moriana tried to calm her heart as she looked to the doorway. She felt her sister approaching, and knew that she was about to learn her fate. She was not fool enough to imagine for an instant that Synalon had denied her to Rann out of any mercy.

If Synalon will not allow Rann to torture me, the princess thought, *what horror does she have in mind?*

". . . but for the really jaded taste, as I perceive Your Majesty's to be," a voice was saying as the stately Synalon came into view, "the sensations to be had from sexual congress with the male of the kine kept by the farmers of the city-states, the so-called hornbulls, cannot be matched."

Looking neither right nor left at the implements of torture, Synalon entered the chamber. She wore a gown

of crimson silk, slit to reveal flashes of creamy thigh
as she walked. She held Erimenes's jug in the crook
of her arm. Her eyebrows were arched in a look of
feigned shock.

"Hornbulls? My dear sage, whatever makes you
think I'd consider such bestiality?"

"Recall that a beast may carry a greater load than
any man, particularly in his loins."

From the corner of her eye, Moriana saw Rann
blush.

"I can't see why you allow this demon to speak so
familiarly to you, my queen," he said stiffly.

Erimenes sputtered.

"He's not a demon, Rann," Synalon said, laughing.
"He's but a ghost. And I do not mind his speech. In
truth, it makes my loins tingle, and I almost wish his
spirit were cloaked in flesh. What might a man learn of
love after fourteen hundred years?"

"Thirteen hundred and ninety-nine," the spirit said
pedantically. "Had I a body, O Queen, I doubt even
I could teach you. The way you served those soldiers
in the barracks, six at one time! Phenomenal. Still," he
went on unctuously, "I'm sure Prince Rann, wise though
he is, cannot fully appreciate such—"

Rann went the color of Synalon's gown. "Were
your spirit clothed in flesh, demon, I'd teach you more
about pain than ever Synalon could of rutting! When
my cousin is done with you—"

"Enough!" Synalon's voice cracked like a lash. She
turned to her sister, who sat listening without interest
to the byplay. "Moriana, beloved sibling, rejoice! I
have consulted the stars, and they bode well. Glorious
destiny shall be yours."

"What are you talking about?" she asked, fighting
the dread that threatened to fill her mind with madness.

Could she? She wondered wildly. *No, it cannot be! Not even Synalon would dare such a thing.*

But as soon as her sister parted lips to speak, she knew it was so.

"I speak of the Rite of Dark Assumption, sister dear, left unperformed these past five thousand years," Synalon said.

"No!" Moriana shrieked. The word rang as though all the agony suffered in this room in thirty millenia had condensed inside her. "No, *no, NO!"*

Synalon's laugh rolled around the chamber. Rann smiled hugely, in admiration and anticipation.

"Say," Erimenes said, "will someone have the courtesy to explain the joke?"

"Synalon!" the captive princess screamed. "You can't mean it! To disturb the demon after so long—do you think you can control it? *Do you?"*

"I have learned much that our weak mother turned from knowing." From a mask of inhuman exultation, Synalon's face became that of a crusader, stern and righteous. "Too long has the Sky City hidden its greatness. To think that for five millenia the most that our magic has accomplished has been the summoning of tame salamanders to light the pleasure palaces of fat bankers in Tolviroth Acerte! Our people cry out for a return to the greatness that was ours when we cast the damned reptiles from our city, and the groundlings shrank in terror from the shadows of our warbirds. Only the dark wisdom of Istu can win us back our power."

Moriana stared at her. Her features were as white and stiff as sunbleached bone. "What if you can't control it? Humans never truly dominated the spawn of the Dark Ones, and the Rite of Dark Assumption has been lost for generations! How do you know that you won't destroy the city instead of bringing back its greatness?"

"Perhaps I don't." Synalon smiled. "What does it matter to you? You'll not know it, sister dear. Your soul will be joined with Istu's in unholy matrimony, after he's worked his will upon your wretched flesh."

"This sounds interesting," Erimenes said.

The black-haired princess ignored him. "Two days," she said. "In two days the stars will be right for Istu to receive his bride. Prepare yourself for your groom, sister mine. The nuptial hour approaches." With Erimenes's jug tucked under her arm, she left.

"My lady." Rann's voice stopped her in the doorway. "Two days is a long time. I fear the hours will weigh heavily upon her."

Synalon scowled impatiently. "What is it you want, cousin?"

"I can lighten the waiting for her." He held up his hand to forestall a furious outburst. "I know ways to, ah, *amuse* Her Highness without working any harm on her body." He smiled wickedly. "Trust me."

"Trust you?" Synalon sniffed derisively. "Do you take me for a fool?" Rann did not answer. He stood stock still regarding her with his eerie, pale eyes.

Synalon felt that anticipation would be the most exquisite torture her sister could possibly endure. But Rann was more than an able servant, he was the best military mind in the Sky City. Her future plans required his skill and cooperation. She wouldn't get them if she thwarted his desires too often.

"Very well," she said with a sigh. "Do as you wish. But I warn you, Rann, do not damage her." She paused, pursing her lips in thought. "You are of royal blood, my cousin," she purred. "I wonder if Istu would be wroth if you took Moriana's place?"

Rann stared at her, and she had the satisfaction of

seeing the flicker of an emotion in his eyes that was normally alien to him. It was good to remind him that she could still make him fear.

"It's something to think about," she said. "Come, Erimenes. There are no hornbulls in the city, but perhaps a stud from the kennels will serve as well. . . ."

In earnest discussion with the dead philosopher, Synalon's voice faded down the corridor until it was lost in its own diminishing echo. Rann's face had recovered its serenity. Rubbing his hands together in a washing motion, he turned to his captive.

High Councillor Uriath was a busy man, and Fost found small cause to complain that he'd been unable to meet with the dignitary the night before—Luranni had produced an astonishing variety of suggestions for activity more diverting. So diverting, in fact, that Fost had no clear memory of the end of the night's festivities. He recalled a sensation of soaring, caused as much by the giddiness of sheer exhaustion as by ecstasy, then a plummet straight into darkness. He remembered nothing of his dreams, but he woke with a vague unease that stayed with him all day. He suspected he'd never sleep untroubled as long as he remained in a city where magic permeated even everyday activities.

Luranni woke long before he did. She looked fresh and unruffled. When he dragged himself to a mirror to shave, he shuddered at the sight. He looked as if he should have been squatting by a campfire in the Thails, with a bone through his nose.

He found water to shave, warm water heated by a captive elemental in the basement of the building. Running water wasn't uncommon in Medurim or Tolviroth, with heated taps available to those who could pay for imported Sky City magic. Such luxury was in short supply on the steppes, however. Fost felt a touch of shame at how much he enjoyed it. Like most Realm-road couriers, he professed a disdain for civilized comforts.

"How do you get the water up here?" he asked, rubbing his face with a towel. "It's heavy to haul up by balloon."

Luranni only smiled. She had grown accustomed to his outlandish ignorance. From a small kitchen on the other side of a beaded curtain came the sounds and smells of cooking, as a servant prepared breakfast. Fost's belly growled like a hungry sled dog.

"We haul some up from the surface," the girl said. "But we are careful about conserving it, and we use our salamanders to distill waste water for use again. Also, we have drains and cisterns to trap rainwater. And, of course, there are the aeroaquifers."

"Ara-what?"

"Aeroaquifers. There are places in the city where water can be brought from the air, as though from an aquifer on land. There are fountains in many streets— I'll show you some today. We don't know how it's done. Magic of the Fallen Ones, you see. My father says we'd work it out fast enough, though, if our rulers paid more mind to practical matters and less to intrigue."

"I thought your father was one of the city's rulers." Fost seated himself on cushions across from Luranni. She wore a shift blazing with color, scarlet, orange, vivid blue. Somehow, the combination did not affront his taste.

"He is an important man, chief of the Council of Advisors. The Council must be consulted on important decisions and is charged with managing the accession of a new monarch when the old one dies—like now. But they cannot make policy."

The curtain parted with a sound like wind through dry branches. The servant entered with that peculiar walk servants accomplish without seeming to move their feet. The servant was a small, wizened person of indeterminate sex, dressed in a shapeless robe. Luranni and her guest were given bowls of steaming, clove-scented tea.

"I don't imagine that sets well with your father," said Fost.

"My father is an ambitious man." Luranni started to sip her tea, halted with the bowl poised beneath her lips. "But his true concern is the welfare of the city, of course."

Fost masked his smile behind his own vessel. Luranni's qualification had come a beat too slow. He wondered what Uriath really had in mind. Yet the underground members he'd met so far had seemed devoted to Moriana. He shrugged and tasted his tea. The hot brew scorched his tongue and tickled it at the same time. He found the effect refreshing.

"When do I meet your father?" Fost asked, feeling impatience begin to prod him again.

"This afternoon, surely," said Luranni.

Fost choked on his tea. "Great Ultimate!" he gagged. The servant reappeared, leathery androgyne face wreathed in steam from plates heaped with food. "What in the name of Ust's claws am I going to do till then?"

Accepting her plate, Luranni said to him, "I'm sure we'll think of something."

Luranni proved no less inventive by daylight than by the soft, steady glow of her lightfool. It was a weak-kneed and somewhat befuddled Fost who set out with her several hours after breakfast for the promised tour of the City in the Sky.

Before they left her apartment, she insisted on disguising him. If the corporal in the orphaned gondola had survived his return to the ground via the guidelines, the Monitors might have a description of the man who had gained entry to the city in such an unorthodox fashion. Fost groaned at the inconvenience. He didn't doubt that the authorities might be looking for him, but he had little confidence in Luranni's concept of what constituted a disguise. He didn't fancy wandering through strange and hostile streets wearing a plaster nose and a bright orange wig.

His fears were unfounded. Luranni produced a black eyepatch.

"Only this?" he asked, skeptical.

"Any seeing you will remember only the eyepatch. None will be able to describe what you really look like." He nodded, remembering his days in Medurim spent as an apprentice cutpurse. His master had insisted that the most effective disguise was also the simplest.

When Fost peered at himself in a mirror, with the patch in place and his cheeks given a gaunt appearance by a shadow drawn below either cheekbone in plain charcoal, he had to admit that no one would mistake the hungry, one-eyed wolf reflected back for Fost Longstrider.

"Raffish," he muttered, not displeased with his new appearance.

"Handsome," said Luranni, smiling. She took his arm, and they left the apartment.

As they wended their way through the tangle of the city's streets, Fost's impressions of the night before were confirmed. The lines of architecture took the eye upward along tapering buildings with peaks hundreds of feet above street-level. It took periodic nudges from Luranni's elbow to keep him from gawking like a hayseed. Nothing would attract unwanted attention faster than acting like an obvious newcomer to the city.

Strangely, the Sky City disconcerted Fost even more by daylight than it had at night. Dark had masked the buildings, revealing only hints of intricate stonework. That had been eerie enough, but the daylight heightened the effect. The proportions of the buildings did not fit themselves to Fost's eye. The balance of space and mass, the flow, the curve, all of it grated. It was wrong only subtly, but still wrong.

His reaction was not mere provincialism. Fost had been in most of the cities of the Realm, seen buildings from the stately colonnades of Medurim to the parti-colored pastel houses scattered among the hills of Kara-Est and the onion-squat domes of Bilsinx and Brev. In the great seaports of the land he had seen embassies and residences built in the fashions of Jorea, the Northern Continent, and even the Far Archipelago in the Antipodes. He'd found some exotic, some amusing, some pleasing, and others not to his taste—but none *disturbing*. Nothing among all the many works of humankind he'd seen affected him the way the city did.

"The works of humankind," he repeated aloud. Luranni looked at him sharply. So did a dozen passersby. While he ruminated, they wandered into a bazaar lined with narrow stalls carved into the facades of buildings.

The answer blazed like a comet in his brain. The City in the Sky was not a "work of humankind". It had been constructed by an alien race thirty thousand years ago. The idea had seemed far-fetched when Luranni had told him the night before. Now it came to him with a force that made him a bit shaky. He had read accounts of the Hissing Ones and the War of Powers and Felarod when he was a youth in High Medurim, and had dismissed them as fantasy. Now, observing the alien architecture of the Sky City, he couldn't deny that some of those fairy tales were true.

"Good day, excellents," a voice said. "Would it

please you to pamper your palates with such delicacies as I have to offer?"

A ginger-eyed youth with hair like a bonfire stood behind one of the graven stone counters. Its bins .overflowed with fruit. Fost looked at him, surprised at how good the offer sounded.

"Would you like some?" asked Luranni.

He nodded. "I've been on the road for weeks. It's hard to get fresh fruit in the south. But isn't it late in the season for fruit?"

"Yes, quite." Luranni picked up a three-lobed yellow fruit and held it up for Fost's inspection. Out of the shade of the booth, its surface showed moist mottlings. "We get them packed in snow, but they don't keep forever. How much for this bedraggled specimen, Herech?"

"For one of your discriminating tastes, Lady Luranni, eleven klenor." Fost blinked. He was no stranger to haggling, but the price was higher than the central spire of the Palace of the Clouds.

"If this *spinas* wasn't so elderly, it might be worth it," she said, tossing the fruit back into the bin. "Come now, Herech, you know better than to toy with me in this fashion. Don't embarrass me before my friend. Give us something worthwhile."

"For you, then," the boy said. He turned into the recesses of the stall and came back with a tray halffilled with melting snow. A globe the size of two fists rested in a cone of white snow. It was pale blue in color, with a silvery sheen that made it as iridescent as a butterfly's wing.

"What's this, Herech? It's lovely!" Luranni exclaimed.

"Unique," the youth said proudly. "A magical hybrid, raised in the hothouse of a Wirixer horticulture mage."

Fost raised an eyebrow. Wirix had no arable land, being located on an island in the midst of Lake Wir at the top of the Quincunx. With the perversity for which they were noted, the Wirixers made an obsession of cultivation. Their savants had developed techniques of growing plants without soil; their mages devoted themselves to creating new and ever more wondrous varieties of plants. Wirix decorative plants, whether miniature trees small enough to flourish on tabletops or shrubs that produced blossoms the size of shields, were valued around the world. A new Wirixer fruit would be a treasure, indeed.

"What do you ask for it?" inquired Luranni, her eyes gleaming at the sight of the fruit.

"A mere hundred klenor."

Fost almost choked at that. A "mere" hundred klenor was a contradiction in terms. Fost earned that for a month's work as courier, and he was among the highest-paid couriers in the Realm. It would buy the favors for the night of a Tolviroth courtesan of the second class, and perhaps even one of the first class if she were not engaged with a ranking banker or corporate head; or a hauberk of heavy scale armor of the type favored by the cataphracts of the Highgrass Broad. To hear such a princely sum mentioned as the price for a piece of fruit made Fost's head spin.

As he stood open-mouthed, Luranni haggled Herech down to eighty klenor, a price for which Fost could have bribed the Bishop of Thrishnoor to denounce the Doctrine of Imminent Confabulation. Her hand darted into the pouch hung from her belt, emerging to rain a brief shower of gold onto the counter in front of Herech. Almost reverently, the youth picked up the fruit and presented it to her.

She broke it in two, handing a piece to Fost. He stared at it, numbed at the prospect of putting three

weeks' wages into his mouth, chewing it, then swallowing it. Luranni bit into her half. The flesh within glowed
translucent and pink, with yellow veins prominent.

Fost took a bite. The meat dissolved on his tongue
into a flavor of sweetness and smoke with a tart edge
that kept it from being cloying. Before he knew it, he
had devoured the entire piece. Young Herech hadn't
lied. The flavor was unique. Never had he known a
fruit so luscious.

"Thank you," he said to Luranni.

"It was worth the price?" she asked needlessly. She
turned and started walking up the street. Fost followed
her but not before he caught a comradely wink from
Herech.

It stopped him in midstride. He realized that Herech
thought the highborn, successful, and lovely merchant
had imported a strapping groundling barbarian to amuse
herself. An initial upwelling of anger gave way to
sheepish amusement. It wasn't all that far from the
truth, and it was a role Fost had played before.

He winked back and set off at a long, loping pace.

"Our prices are high," Luranni confessed, waving at
the stalls laden with colorful goods of every description.
"But everything must be imported. Raised up from the
surface by balloon. In fact, we're going now to the
cargo docks on the starboard side of the city."

" 'Starboard?' "

"The city changes directions every time it arrives at
a juncture of the Quincunx. To say something is on the
north side and something on the west makes little sense
when the bearings change every few weeks. Here we
have port and starboard, and fore and aft, just as you
do on a seafaring ship. In a way, that's what we are,
a ship that sails the sky."

They left the street of merchants, turned a corner
and found themselves by one of the compact clear

spaces dotted around the city. A fountain in the center arched water from the mouth of a monster with sideways-hinged jaws into a wide, shallow stone basin. Luranni touched Fost's arm and nodded toward the odd fountain.

"An aeroaquifer."

Fost swallowed hard, uneasy at the sight. It felt as if tiny insects crawled over his flesh, and the cut across his back seemed to pucker and bind. Water springing from thin air disconcerted him. The idea that even the adepts of the City of Sorcery failed to understand how the aeroaquifer worked frightened him even more.

They walked on. Sky Citizens passed them in both directions, going about their business. Watching them, Fost noted that they almost scurried, as if they were afraid it was about to rain. In the sounds of bargaining at the bazaar he'd heard a slightly shrill note; he put the two observations together and realized that the residents of the city, as much as they tried to hide it, were very, very scared.

From what Luranni had told him about the candidate for their next queen, Fost didn't blame them.

Luranni alone seemed unaffected by the fear. He reflected that she probably felt her position as daughter of High Councillor Uriath protected her from harm. All of the underground youths he'd seen the day before looked well-born. They probably all harbored similar feelings. It certainly accounted for the lack of skill at clandestine activity. They didn't—couldn't—take it seriously. It was only a game they played, in which the stakes were no more than embarrassment and inconvenience should they lose.

Fost hoped Luranni wouldn't learn the truth the hard way. It would almost certainly be Prince Rann who would teach her.

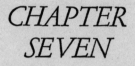

*CHAPTER
SEVEN*

"I don't wish to be pessimistic," High Councillor Uriath intoned, "but our chances of rescuing the Princess Moriana are slim. Very slim." He shook his great white-fringed head with ponderous regret.

Seeing Fost's scowl, Luranni squeezed his hand. The courier grunted and glanced across the table. For the first time since he'd entered the wine warehouse, led blindfolded to this rendezvous by Luranni, Fost wasn't the object of Erlund's hate-filled glare. The straw-haired youth frowned at Uriath instead.

Luranni confirmed what Fost had already surmised. Young Erlund was of the city's petty nobility, almost as far below Moriana in rank as was the slum-bred courier. That hadn't kept him from falling in love with her.

Fost welcomed this alliance in urging Moriana's rescue. The meeting in the murky storeroom, surrounded by tar-sealed casks of wine, was composed half of men and women Fost's age and half of men like Uriath, lords and merchants of advanced years. Despite the gap in ages, the mood was almost unanimous; the sour smell of wine and pessimism hung thick in the air.

"You see, young man," Uriath said, leaning toward Fost, "the princess has, beyond doubt, been under questioning by Prince Rann for hours. We can only assume that she's told her captors anything they wish to know."

"That's a lie!" Erlund boiled to his feet, shaking with

rage, his face as red as the High Councillor's. "Moriana wouldn't tell those scum a thing!"

"Don't be a groundling, Erlund," a voice growled from the dimness that filled the storeroom despite the bright morning outside. "Rann could make the Vicar of Istu confess to worshipping Felarod. She's sung like a raven in mating time by now, you can bet your last sipan."

Erlund dropped into his seat as though stunned by a mighty blow. Fost's eyes widened. The name "Rann" must hold powerful magic if it could quench Erlund so easily.

"Who is this Rann, anyway?" he demanded. "The mere mention of his name makes everyone goggle as if they're about to birth a whale."

"You don't know of Rann?" a girl asked, incredulous at such ignorance. Fost shook his head.

"Rann is prince of the city, first cousin to Synalon and Moriana," Luranni explained, pitching her voice low as if afraid that speaking the prince's name might cause him to appear in a puff of brimstone. "His mother was Ekrimsin the Ill-Favored, as unlike her sister Derora as Synalon is unlike Moriana. He was always a wild and unmanageable child, but not uncommonly so. He showed an early aptitude for war.

"Then he led an expedition against the tribesmen who plague the passes through the Thail Mountains. An accident crippled his war-bird; he landed alone and was captured. His men found him and rescued him. But not before the Thailint had burned away his manhood with a torch."

Fost shuddered. Rann might be a fiend straight from Hell, but Fost could pity anyone who'd undergone such an ordeal.

"His spirit was warped," Uriath said. "Denied more natural outlets for his passion, he vents his lust in torture, to which he brings all the intelligence and imagination of the Etuul line." He puffed himself up slightly at the mention of the dynasty. Luranni had mentioned to Fost the night before that her line traced descent from an Etuul monarch.

"So not only is it likely that Moriana has revealed everything she knows about your underground, but that . . ." He paused, testing the flavor of possible ways of phrasing it, and liking none. ". . . that, in her present condition, the princess might not conceive it a favor to be rescued. I fear that all she desires now is the palliative only death can bring."

The silence grew more dense than the wine-smell. Fost's mind spun. *If Moriana dies, I'll never find Erimenes,* he thought. But worse was another thought, like a spear of ice in his gut: the woman with whom he'd lain beneath the stars might soon be reduced to a shapeless, broken thing that wept blood from eyeless sockets and mewled for death. Sweat cascaded down his forehead, stinging his eyes.

The door swung open. The conspirators gasped as one. By the time the interloper had fully entered the storeroom, Fost stood with curved blade in hand, ready to take out his rage and frustration in hot blood.

But it was another young conspirator, whom Fost recognized from the night before. "Soldiers," he said. "A troop of them just coming down the street."

Uriath paléd. The conspirators all began to talk at once.

"Hold on a moment," Fost said. The panicky clamor mounted. He slammed the pommel of his sword against the table. "*Hold,* dammit! And keep the noise down, or we're lost for sure."

The noise subsided. He turned to the frightened messenger. "Now tell me, are these bird riders or the Monitors everyone fears so?"

"Common soldiers of the watch."

Fost nodded. "And would Synalon dispatch such dross to arrest the High Councillor?"

He didn't know if she would or not, but he knew that if the conspirators' fears weren't soothed, they'd bolt into the street like frightened cattle. If, by some chance, the soldiers hadn't already guessed something was amiss, that would give them the idea soon enough.

"You are right, boy," Uriath said, straightening unconsciously. "You, Testin, go and watch them. If they approach the warehouse, give the alarm. But be certain." The youth bobbed his head and disappeared.

If Fost had ever lived longer minutes than the ones which followed, he'd long since forgotten them. Every eye in the dank chamber fixed on him. The wait sparked the certainty that he'd guessed wrong. In spite of Uriath's vanity, the dark princess had sent low-caste troops to bring him to account. In a moment the doors would burst apart, the room would fill with men, and Fost Longstrider, outlander and courier, would shortly learn all he'd care to about Prince Rann's personality quirks.

The door burst open. It was only Testin, carrying a sheet of birdskin parchment in trembling hands.

"They nailed this to the front of the storehouse across the way and went on," he said. He passed the sheet to Uriath. The High Councillor squinted, held it at arm's length, and scanned it rapidly.

"This changes things," he said. " 'Be it proclaimed: tomorrow at the fifth hour after dawn, the false traitor Moriana is, for the crimes of regicide, matricide, and treason, to be sacrificed to Holy Istu for the good of the city. With this seal confirmed, Synalon, Queen.' "

"The Rite of Dark Assumption!" Luranni breathed.

"Lies!" Erlund shouted. "She would not dare!"

Everyone ignored him. Uriath's eyes were as huge

as his daughter's. "We must act," he said. "We must free the princess. The Rite must not take place. If Synalon gains the demon's power, we are doomed."

"I thought it would be no favor to rescue Moriana," Fost asked.

Uriath shook his head. "I was wrong. Rann won't have touched her. The Bride of Istu must be unsullied when she goes to the Vicar."

If that means she has to be a virgin, Moriana is going to disappoint the Vicar, whomever he might be. Fost almost reeled at the impact of returning hope.

"You must help us," said Uriath.

"Not so fast," Fost said. "I've no interest in your civil affairs. All I'm interested in is getting back my parcel."

Uriath frowned. "You'll get your parcel back. If you help us free Moriana, you can have any parcel in the city. You can have my whole trade stock if you so desire, wine, salamanders, everything."

"Salamanders?" Fost asked.

The High Councillor gestured irritably. "Of course. I own a concession to export small fire elementals under spells of obedience. They're our main item of trade." Uriath allowed himself a rueful smile. "The prevalence of the sprites is one reason Rann's found it so easy to use them against us."

"All I want is the property I'm to deliver," Fost stated with absolute honesty. "If you can guarantee me that, I'll help you as best I can."

"Done." A hint of suspicion lurked in Uriath's blue eyes. Did he wonder at the courier's determination to risk the wrath of Synalon and Rann merely to regain a parcel? Fost didn't delude himself that the question would fail to occur to the Councillor. He only hoped that the pressures of the crisis kept Uriath's mind from worrying the puzzle too hard.

"One more thing," Fost said as the meeting began to dissolve. Fost held up his short Sky City scimitar. "You need me to fight for you, and I'd rather work with the type of blade I'm accustomed to. Have you any broadswords in stock, or do you know where I can get one?"

"Yes," Uriath responded, his brow creasing as he thought. "I have one that may suffice. Luranni will see that it reaches you before tomorrow. Go now. My daughter will show you what you must know to plan the rescue. We'll meet tonight to plan further." He looked at Luranni for a moment. "Take good care of him, Luranni."

"I will, Father," she said innocently. Turning, the older man missed the look she gave the courier.

The girl screamed as the whip bit her flesh.

Moriana's scream rose with hers, scarcely less agonized, though the princess was untouched. "Catannia!" she cried. "Oh, Holy Ones, why is this happening?" The girl whimpered. Moriana didn't know whether the pitiful noise was a response to her cry or just a mindless protest against pain. The brutal caress of the many-thonged whip had changed the lovely, active girl Moriana had played with as a child into a mass of shredded, bloody rags of flesh hung from the ceiling of the dungeon.

His hands clasped behind him, rocking slightly on the balls of his feet, Prince Rann cocked his head toward Moriana. "You invoke those heretics' gods on the eve of your wedding to Istu? How droll." A wheeled black brazier smoldered near him, cradling white-hot instruments to await his pleasure. The glow turned his face into a demon's visage. "If you must know why your friend suffers, it is through your own evil in turning traitor to the Sky City. Treason is contagious, you know. You were raised with this slut and doubtless infected her with your sedition. We must purge this sickness, wipe it out before it spreads." With a splendidly helpless gesture, he turned to the burly guards who flanked the suspended girl. The whips sang again.

The smell of blood filled Moriana's nostrils like molten copper. Rann's eyes moved restlessly from her to Catannia and back, as the whips made the nude, dangling body rotate slowly. Moriana winced at every stroke.

Had she had room in her mind, she would have marked how her sister's power had solidified. Catannia's father was a minor noble of some influence among the aristocracy of the city. It was a bold stroke to have the daughter seized and subjected to torture for no more than lifelong friendship with the Princess Moriana. Yet it was a clever move, adding weight to the spurious claims of Moriana's treason.

But Moriana's mind was overcrowded with horror. Not even thought of her impending degradation by the Vicar of Istu could force its way past the knowledge that she was responsible for her friend's agony.

Under a new onslaught, Catannia's cries had grown perceptibly weaker. Now, as both whips gouged at what had been her buttocks, the cries ceased altogether. Rann frowned.

"Rouse her," he commanded, irked that his sport had been interrupted.

The soldiers laid down their whips, fetched buckets of icy water and threw them over the limp figure. Catannia did not stir. The treatment was repeated without success. Then a soldier laid his head to the girl's ribs, beneath the flaccid ruin of her breasts.

"My lord," he quavered, "her heart has stopped."

Rann sneered. "A weakling. Such creatures are better

off dead. There will be no room for weaklings in the new dawn of the city's glory." he sighed. "Well, Darman and Krydlach, why are you loitering? Bring in the next traitor to atone for his malfeasance."

The guards went out, then returned supporting between them what Moriana thought to be a skeleton somehow imbued with a ghastly semblance of life. But though it couldn't stand unaided, its gaunt head was held high. Something in its carriage struck Moriana as familiar.

The head turned toward her. The sockets were empty, running thin streams of blood. The face was disfigured with half-healed burns—but the princess knew it.

"Kralfi," she said, not loudly but in a shocked whisper, as if speaking the name quietly she could deny the reality facing her. The mouth that had smiled down on her in her crib was a jagged hole rimmed with stumps of teeth. Fingers that had frequently stroked her cheek with paternal affection hung limp as worms, their bones smashed almost to powder. To a princess barred by tradition from ever seeing her father or learning his name, Chamberlain Kralfi had been a beloved substitute.

He had also been the chief of Moriana's personal spy network, her best hope of countering Synalon's ambition. All hope was shattered now, shattered with the loyal old retainer's joints.

Rann smiled at his cousin's expression. "I regret that we had already entertained the excellent Kralfi for some time before your apprehension. But now that you're here, dear cousin, I've arranged a most suitable . . ."

"Jackal!" The voice that cut through Rann's was garbled by the old man's wrecked mouth, but it cracked with authority, defiance and pride. "Save your childish torments, half-man. I have failed my lady. That's punishment more dreadful than any your feeble wit can devise.

"Forgive me, my princess," the ghastly visage said.

Moriana forced words past an obstruction in her throat. "I forgive you." It seemed to her that the torn lips formed a smile. Then the old man pitched, face forward, to the floor and lay unmoving.

Rann knelt by his side. Kralfi was as dead as Catannia. His heart had not been weak, merely old; already he had suffered torture sufficient to kill a man of lesser resolve. Will alone had kept him alive long enough to seek Moriana's absolution.

Rann turned livid. He clenched his fists beside his cheeks and squalled with fury. "Cheated!" he screamed in shrill tones. "Twice cheated! But not again!"

He took personal charge of torturing a string of victims like a procession of memories from Moriana's past: her ancient serving-maid, her fencing master, the sages who'd tutored her in arcane lore, other playmates. His hand wielded the scalpel that sliced, the heated pincers that tore, the ladle that dripped molten lead into mouths and eye-sockets and other orifices. In the detached voice he used when most caught up with the elation of pain-giving, he informed the princess that he'd even have tortured her war-bird Ayoka before her eyes, except that the eagle had disappeared from the royal aerie.

"Doubtless he died unnoticed and alone, and fell from the city for the scavengers to gnaw his bones," the prince said, as he slit open a shrieking serving-maid with surgical exactness.

Through it all, Moriana felt every pang suffered by her friends and loved ones. Synalon had been wrong and Rann horribly right: being made to witness the final agonies of those she held dear was infinitely worse than merely waiting her tryst with the Demon of the Dark Ones.

With a raucous cry and a flurry of wings, a raven entered the small opening near the top of the arched window. It fluttered down to perch on a shelf laden with books. Beside it rested the bust of an ancient poet. The statue seemed to be contemplating the feathered invader of his sanctuary with quizzical interest.

Moriana slumped in a chair. The nightlong ordeal had left her exhausted, physically, spiritually, and emotionally. The raven cocked its head at her, regarding her from small, bright, evil eyes. With a derisive caw, it took off and flew back out the window, unwilling to associate with one already condemned.

After Rann had finished his grisly entertainment, Synalon had ordered her sister conveyed to the rooms she had once occupied in the palace. For the moment, the captive had allowed herself a frayed wisp of joy, if not actual hope. Some unacknowledged scrap of decency must exist in Synalon, if she was willing to let Moriana lighten her final hours by a return to the chambers that had been home for most of her life.

Guards had escorted her into the tower nearer the leading edge of the city, and then pushed open the door. Moriana saw inside and knew she was a fool.

Of all her sister's aberrations, Moriana found few less palatable than Synalon's preoccupation with her poison-taloned ravens. The beasts were a sorry contrast to the lordly war-eagles of the Sky City. Filthy, craven, unmannered things they were, eaters of carrion and the lice that swarmed through their matted ebon feathers. They imitated human speech, but that made them more disgusting to the golden-haired princess. Their clacking, wheezing conversation sounded like crude parody of a consumptive.

Synalon had not allowed Moriana's chambers to rest idle in the months since she had departed the city in her quest for Erimenes and the amulet. Synalon had converted them to a mew for her reeking pets.

The door opened. Moriana looked up listlessly. Synalon stood in the door, clad conservatively in a deep gray and ochre wrap belted firmly against the chill. Her pale skin glowed with its own luminescence in dawn light the color of soured milk.

"Good morrow, sister," Synalon said softly.

Moriana ignored her. She turned away. Her eyes brushed shelves bowed under the weight of cracked and ancient tomes of history, poetry, sorcerous lore. Shelves and books alike were fouled and streaked with the white excrement of Synalon's ravens. Moriana stared at the bare stone floor and wondered if despair could be more complete than hers.

"No kind words for me, your beloved sister?" Synalon glided in and sat in a chair facing her captive. The door closed quietly. Moriana did not doubt that a score of guards waited outside, poised to lunge through to the rescue at the first sound of trouble. Fit though she was, Synalon lacked her sister's skill at physical combat, armed or otherwise.

Yet Synalon's mere presence was a flaunting of her own superiority. Face to face with her sister, Moriana would not have the least chance to outmatch her in a test of magic. Moriana's skills were great, her powers sharply honed, but interest and temperament had led her to the pursuit of bright magic, healing magic, that magic bringing peace and plenty. Synalon had steeped herself in the lore of the Dark Ones. She glanced death, and gestured with thunderbolts; her destructiveness was as invincible to Moriana as it was alien.

The Amulet of Living Flame would have changed that invincibility. With the Athalar magic to restore her life, she could weather the hellstorm of Synalon's deathbolts. With luck she could draw on the life force within the amulet to add power to her own conjurings.

"You should not have returned," said Synalon.

Moriana paled, holding in a breath of air tainted by the sharp, stale-sweet stink of the ravens.

"You wished to see our dear mother again, didn't you? You felt concern over her health." Synalon's lips curled. "Sentiment was always your weakness, my darling sister."

"You may be right."

Laughing, Synalon rose, walked to stand beside her sister. Moriana did not turn. She tensed as Synalon laid hands on her shoulders but made no sound.

"You wish to know of Queen Derora's last hours?" asked Synalon. "How she died, and if her last thoughts were of you?"

"Of course."

Synalon began to knead her sister's shoulders. Icy feathers brushed along Moriana's spine.

"Our mother had not been well for quite some time. Her condition was not improved by the way you vanished in the middle of the night without a word for those who loved you. I think she entered her final decline with the news that you'd gone."

Moriana tried to guard against heeding her sister's words. Yet they touched a guilt that had burdened her since her last departure from the city. She had abandoned her mother in the queen's final illness—abandoned her to the tender attentions of a daughter who hated her.

"She died badly. There was much pain." Synalon made no attempt to hide the relish she felt mouthing those words. Moriana went bowstring-taut with the sudden impulse to lash out, to strike down her sister.

With a quicksilver peal of laughter, Synalon glided

back. "Transparent as always, sibling," she said mockingly. "Will you never learn? You cannot compete with me."

"What did Derora die of?" asked Moriana. "She had sickened before I left, but the doctors offered no cause."

"No mystery there. It was of a poison most subtle."

Moriana's head snapped around. Synalon giggled with girlish delight at her expression of horror. "You lie," Moriana said in a dead voice. "Not that I doubt your capacity for such vileness. But Derora was wily, more than either of us. She could scent any venom-brew you could concoct before your hand finished conjuring it."

"Quite true. So my hand never concocted it. It was instead prepared by the hand of an Elder Brother of the Brethren of Assassins, and used to permeate a stole sent by Emperor Teom of High Medurim to mark the anniversary of his conception."

Dizziness whirled within Moriana. Though she knew her sister must have murdered their mother, still she dreaded admitting it. If even Derora was powerless to stop Synalon, Moriana could hold out little hope for besting her sister.

"She had the Sensitivities," Moriana said. "She could have detected any substance in lethal concentrations."

"In lethal concentration," Synalon said, nodding. "But not in a dose nicely tailored to sicken, without being potent enough to kill. Similar dosages pushed her nearer to earshot of Hell Call. It took time, Istu knows; our mother was as cunning as a bitch-fox with a lair of kits. But I'm the bitch's bitch-kit, and am cunning, too."

"Who gave her the poison? She would never trust you."

"True, nor Rann or any of my retainers. But she trusted Kralfi."

Had Moriana eaten she would have vomited. Kralfi,

who was tortured to death not seven hours before, had died proclaiming his fealty. She didn't believe Synalon.

Synalon watched her closely, shrugged and spoke. "You'd divine the truth soon enough, so I shall tell you. He did not know. He thought he was bringing his queen a present of great beauty and value. She stroked over it, the poison insinuated itself through the pores in her skin, and slowly she died." Synalon laughed. "Did you say something?"

"Yes," Moriana said, almost inaudibly. "I asked, did he know?"

"Of course. Rann told him—later. Watching his reaction gave our cousin the most exquisite pleasure, I'm sure. Dear Rann must have almost recalled what ejaculation feels like."

Moriana sat unmoving, unspeaking. Sadness for a mother murdered and a loyal servant who died knowing he had helped murder her crowded out all thought of her own impending doom.

"So," she said at length, "Derora the Wise succumbed to poison. A shabby end for a great monarch."

"But she did not die of poison." Moriana looked up, eyes wide with surprise.

"You said . . ."

"Yes, we weakened her with poison. But, Istu gnaw her entrails, she hung on in spite of all we did. We pushed the quantities of the toxin as high as we could without alerting her. I think she had magics of her own that helped her cling to life so tenaciously."

"How did my mother die?" demanded Moriana.

"Why, I smothered her with a pillow."

With an eagle's cry of killing rage, Moriana launched herself from the chair. Synalon's moon-pale skin turned the color of a waterlogged corpse. She leaped back, stumbled and struck the floor in a tangle of slender limbs and expensive cloth.

A frantic heave took her out of her sister's path. Then she was on her feet, interposing a writing table between her and Moriana. Moriana wrenched it from her and threw it away with such force that the hardwood broke like glass against the wall. Her fingers sought Synalon's throat.

But Synalon's lips moved rapidly. Moriana heard no words above the roaring of her own pulse. Her nails touched skin. Then a light exploded in the center of her brain.

Strength fled her limbs. She fought to stay on her feet, to keep her arms reaching out for her sister's life. A yellow glow surrounded her like fog, growing brighter in gradual pulses. Her legs gave way. She dropped to her knees not even feeling the pain as they raked along the floor.

Synalon loomed over her. The black-haired enchantress's shape wavered like an elemental. Moriana blinked. Her stomach surged with nausea.

"Sometimes I despair of you, sister," said Synalon. "You never learn." She turned and walked to the door.

Once there she paused to look back. "Your strength will return in a short while. My little spell did you no permanent harm. We can't have you ill on your wedding day, can we?"

She danced out through the door. Moriana felt sensation return to her limbs in a many-pointed prickling. The sickness in her stomach subsided slowly.

But even when the paralysis had left her, Moriana did not weep. It was not courage that kept her eyes dry; it was simply that her state transcended tears.

A wind sharp with autumn chill whipped across the Circle of the Skywell, scattering small bits of rubbish. Fost held the bulky cloak close about him, grateful for its warmth as well as its concealment. The air was

noticeably cooler here, a thousand feet above the
prairie.

Few people stirred. Those whom Fost and Luranni
encountered ducked their heads and hurried by without
so much as a greeting or a glance. The grip of fear had
clamped the city's heart.

Luranni's great golden eyes moved constantly, alert
for the purple tabards and black breastplates of the
Monitors, the dread police instituted by Rann. Seemingly, they were as much under the spell of tension as
ordinary citizens. Luranni and Fost had seen a squad of
them a few blocks away, but they had gone on without
challenging the pair.

For the hundredth time, Fost dropped his hand to
the reassuring feel of his new broadsword in a bird-
leather scabbard swinging at his hip. Uriath had done
well by him. The new sword was a far better weapon
than the one which had gone into the fumarole with
the faceless ape-thing in Kest-i-Mond's castle. Broad
and wide of blade, the sword was lightened by a wide
blood gutter, and tapered to a serviceable point. Its
blued-steel basket hilt protected the hand that gripped
it without restricting the wrist. The High Councillor's
daughter told him he'd have small need for it today.
His height made him conspicuous, but the merchant-
nobles often employed big outlanders for their personal
guard.

Fost could see why. Aside from the elite bird riders
and the royal family itself, the Sky Citizens didn't seem
a prepossessing lot. The tall courier was only too aware
of the limitations of his own co-conspirators. Leaders
and followers alike came from the aristocracy, which
was comprised of merchant princes such as Uriath and
his leisure-loving friends. They might be adroit at
convoluted palace intrigues, but they were innocents
in the gutter-fighting realities of insurrection. Fost had

ample evidence of their clumsiness, and he knew that
the reason they were so eager for his aid was that they
had no other swordsmen of any skill. Fost doubted that
the lithe girl walking beside him knew which end of a
sword to use. He couldn't help contrasting her with
Moriana.

Moriana!

Tomorrow would tell whether he lost her to some
awful fate none had yet fully explained to him. With
her would go all hope of immortality. His only allies
would be dilettantes and amateurs who knew nothing
of stealth, security or battle. They'd lost Moriana within
a few hours of her arrival; Fost had seen through their
clumsy attempt at a trap even as it was being set; and
this very morning a knot of soldiers out tacking up
Synalon's proclamation had thrown Uriath's underground into desperate panic.

Nervously, he fingered his sword. He almost wished
someone would challenge him. Then he could quench
his anxieties in the hot rush of action.

Their steps carried them along the cleared circle
around the well itself. In ancient days, Luranni informed
him, the People had used the vast opening to focus
Demon Istu's powers against opponents below. Now
the Skywell was mostly used for the purpose of
"exiling" undesirables.

Fost's eyes kept returning to the palace, several
hundred yards distant along a wide, white avenue. The
structure bulked huge, yet its construction was so airy,
spun of arches and flying buttresses, that it gave the
impression of weightlessness. Fost wasn't deceived. He
knew enough of fortification to see that, for all its
baroque appearance, it'd be a formidable citadel to
assault.

Something in the way the light struck the avenue
running from the palace brought him to a halt. The

paving seemed to be large, round rocks set in some black substance. The curious cobbling ended before the avenue joined the circle and was cordoned by almost invisible threads strung between brass posts.

"Magic barrier?" Fost asked. Luranni nodded. "Why?"

"None but the feet of royalty may walk upon the skulls of past queens," the girl replied.

"Skulls?"

"Yes. When a ruler of the city dies, her skull becomes another paving stone, set in pitch among the skulls of her mothers." Luranni spoke with the atonal solemnity she always used when discussing the history and traditions of the city. Fost wondered if she were reciting litanies taught her by her father.

He couldn't help shuddering as he looked at the Skullway. The Hissing Folk might have been defeated long ago, but they had left their legacy. Thirty thousand years of grim evil had steeped the very stones of the city.

They walked on, skulls and palace burning in Fost's mind. "Don't take offense," he said, "but your father strikes me as the ambitious type. Why doesn't he forget about saving Moriana and try to seize power himself?"

Luranni laughed. "None but a woman may hold sovereignty in the city. So it is written. The people wouldn't accept a male ruler, fearing it would rob the city of the magic that makes it float."

Fost's stomach turned over. He'd managed to forget that he'd spent almost a day on a platform of stone that hung a thousand feet off the ground with no visible means of support. The firmness beneath his feet suddenly seemed to pitch and roll like a ship on storm-tossed waters. The gusting breeze threatened to overturn the vast sky-raft and dash him to destruction. He had meant to ask Luranni why her father didn't try to put her on the throne, but for a few minutes it was all he could do to keep from hurling himself face-down and clutching the street with desperate fingers. When the fear passed, the question had gone with it.

"Tell me about the Rite of Dark Assumption," he said when he'd mastered himself, looking studiously away from the gold eyes that glinted with amusement. "What does it involve?"

"With much ceremony and incantation, the prin—, the victim is violated by the Vicar of Istu. When that is done, the demon takes her soul."

They had gone past where the Skullway met the Circle and around a quarter of the promenande surrounding the Well. Luranni gestured at a point directly across from the mouth of the Way of Skulls.

"There is the altar where the royal victims are bound."

Fost saw the low, flat slab next to an immense black statue. He pulled on his chin, trying to beat down fear and clear his mind for scheming. "We'll need a diversion," he said, keeping his tone light. "You can't have a rescue without a diversion."

He thought some more. "How is it that your father can keep warehouses full of fire elementals without burning out a whole quarter of the city? To say nothing of how he's managed to avoid Rann's spies."

"I can answer both questions at once. The elementals are small ones, enchanted to obey commands from those unskilled in magic. They're bought for smelters, heating, the kitchens of estates. While they prefer easily burned substances for food, they can burn almost anything at need, and consume it all, with no ash. This makes them in demand among those who can pay our prices." He caught a note of pride in her voice. She served as negotiator with Quincunx city factors on behalf of Uriath's concern. "So they're kept in magicked clay vessels. That holds both them and their heat. It also blinds them to what goes on outside the jars. Those vessels are quite handy. They were invented centuries ago, in Athalau. Spirit jugs, I believe they're called. What's the matter?"

Fost had gulped audibly at the mention of Athalau and spirit jugs. It became doubly important that no member of Uriath's underground ever get so much as a glimpse of Erimenes and his pot. He didn't know how widely the existence of Erimenes and the amulet might be spread. But Kest-i-Mond, Moriana, and Synalon knew, at the very least. It seemed a fair guess that Uriath might, too. If he connected the parcel Fost was so desperate to recover with an Athalar spirit jug . . .

"What?" he said, feigning distraction. "Oh, nothing. I simply felt a moment's trepidation at the thought of the odds we'll be facing tomorrow." He finished with the most wolfish grin he could muster to let Luranni know he felt no trepidation at all. In fact he did, a great deal, but saw no reason she should know.

She smiled back and squeezed his arm. The contact sent a thrill through his body. He hoped he could formulate a rescue plan soon enough to have a few hours alone with Luranni before meeting again with the underground. Already the rudiments of a scheme came to him.

"I think I see how it'll go," he said, grave as a field marshal planning his campaign. "Our larcenous princess is brought forth and bound to the altar. Then this Vicar of Istu has his way with her, right?" The girl nodded. "So the Vicar—the name conjures up a skinny old codger with yesterday's gruel in his beard, and spectacles perched on his nose like a Tolviroth accounting clerk—so he gives Moriana a dose of his withered old prod. That'll be the best time to make our move, when all eyes are on the, ah, main event. I'll make for the

altar with a team of picked men, if we can find any
among your comrades who're more of a menace to
others than to themselves. At the same time, you'll
release a passle of tame salamanders into the crowd,
under orders to make things warm for the onlookers.
Then . . ."

His words dwindled to uneasy silence. He became
aware of large golden eyes fixing him with a peculiar
look. "You don't think that'll work?" he asked plain-
tively. Luranni shook her head. "Why not?"

She pointed once more. They were forty yards from
the altar and the statue looming over it, near enough
to make out detail. Short columns held the marble slab
of the altar, which formed the shape of a Y. Fost
scarcely noticed. The statue was of such uncommon
ugliness that it commanded all his attention.

It squatted, clawed hands resting on basalt knees,
leering down on humans less than half its height. Its
form was manlike, but disproportionately thick of
trunk and limb. Teeth filled its awful grin, blunt and
bone-crushing save for two curving tusks. Nose and
cheeks were wide and flat, eyes slanted beneath great
juts of heavy brow. The whole expression was chillingly
malevolent. Stubby horns curled outward and upward
from either side of its head, an unnatural touch in a
land where horn-bearing creatures wore them on nose
and forehead. Between its thighs hung an immense,
misshapen member of the same dark stone.

"What," Fost said, knowing that Luranni's objec-
tions to his plan were bound up in this monstrosity, "is
that?"

"The Vicar of Istu," she replied.

CHAPTER
EIGHT

Shadows of high clouds fell on Moriana like a weight as her feet paced the uneven yards of the Way of Skulls. A bitter wind whipped her green sacrifical cloak about her legs, causing her to stumble repeatedly.

To either side, the Skullway was lined with jeering multitudes kept at bay by the magic cordon. *Synalon's done her propagandizing well,* the princess thought. Any citizen should have known Moriana was innocent of her mother's murder, the mother whom she admired and Synalon despised. But Moriana's arrival in the city on the heels of Derora's death, and the lies spread by Synalon's agents, had turned the people of the city from sympathy for the blonde princess to rabid hate. Even the repression by Guardsmen and Monitors was laid to Moriana; but for her act of treachery, the rumor mongers said, such stern measures wouldn't have been required.

A gob of spittle hit her cheek. She bit back the soul-frying curse that rose to her lips and kept her eyes from moving to her tormentor in the crowd. She might not die a queen, but she would die like one.

Escorted by halberd-bearing Monitors, Moriana reached the Circle and began the slow procession to the altar. From above, the beat of wings rolled down like thunder. Rann, astride red-crested Terror, led the regiments of the Guard in a sardonic escort of honor.

The raw passion surging from the mob pushed her gaze aside into the gape of the Well itself. Below, land slipped by at a mile an hour. A few puffs of cloud drifted between earth and city. The green hills beneath, already changing to autumn yellow, beckoned the princess.

A brief dash, a leap, a blissful float to Hell Call, she thought. *How much better than the degradation and damnation that awaits me.*

But the hope was no more substantial than the clouds below. Against such an attempt to cheat Istu—and Synalon—the Monitors had been armed with weighted nets.

I'll walk to my fate, and not be carried like some miserable groundling, she vowed to herself.

For all her determination to hold her head erect, she couldn't make her eyes rise to behold the leering Vicar. The phalanx of Monitors snapped to a halt. Moriana raised her gaze.

Her sister stood on the far side of the altar. Her hair was caught up in an intricate coiffure, her body wrapped in a pearl-white robe. The blue eyes glinted with triumph. Moriana felt her knees go weak. It was obvious that Synalon intended to carry through with the unholy ceremony.

Until this instant, some corner of the princess's being had cherished the hope that Synalon's threats to invoke Istu had been no more than that. Surely, not even she would dare disturb the demon. She would torture her sister and cast her over the side to clean oblivion.

But Synalon wore the ceremonial vestments of the Rite, which hadn't been donned in five thousand years.

When she saw the realization in her sister's eyes, Synalon turned and lifted her arms to the crowd. The eager susurration died.

"Hear me, O denizens of the clouds," the sorceress cried. Her words cut across the wind to the city beyond.

"The honor of our domain has been besmirched by an act of treason so vile that my lips hesitate to speak of it." She swept her hand toward her captive. "Behold Moriana, who basely contrived the death of her mother, our queen, to seize the throne for herself!"

A moan of animal rage rolled from the crowd. Moriana's soul shrank from its intensity.

"It is judgment, O citizens." The raven-tressed woman clenched her fists. "That one of us, my own sister, should perpetrate such a deed, shows how far our city has fallen into decay.

"No mortal suffering would be sufficient to punish the murderess of Derora the Wise. Thus do I consign the traitor Moriana to a fate commensurate with her offense, and at the same time turn our noble city's path from decadence to domination.

"Thus do I give Moriana to Istu, the soul of the city, to be his wedded bride throughout eternity!"

A wail rose from ten thousand throats, compounded of eagerness and dismay, of terror and pure, surging lust. Rough hands gripped Moriana, stripping the green robe of shame from her. In her nakedness, she still stood proud, despite the bite of the wind, the voices that cried out to see her ravaged by the demon, the towering nearness of the Vicar. The Monitors, faceless in their bronze masks, drew her out on the altar, clamped her legs wide on the branches of the Y-shaped slab, and tied her wrists above her head.

She saw rather than heard Synalon recite the summoning. She felt the power rising, as if from the very stones. She smelled incense and a sudden stink of decay. At last some magnetism drew her eyes to the basalt ikon that was the Vicar.

Its eyes opened.

* * *

In darkness, its bower roofed in tons of stone, a demon slept.

It had slept thus for millenia. Once, though, it had known freedom. In the youth of the universe it had been created, and in time sent by the Dark Ones, its creators, to their votaries the *Zr'gsz*, to aid them and keep them strong in the cause of evil. Those had been the high days, the days of glory, when the black demon rode his raft of stone across the sky and visited shrieking death upon the foes of the Hissers.

Change.

The Pale Folk, the Ones Below who crawled like maggots across the face of the planet, began to resist. Their efforts were paltry at first, and with orgiastic glee Istu destroyed them. But they learned.

One rose among the Pale Ones, one whose name rang now and again through the sleeping demon's brain in a discord of agony: Felarod.

He had the blessing of the Three and Twenty of Agift, sworn foes throughout eternity of the Lords of the Elder Dark. And more than that, the World-Spirit, very soul of the planet itself, had rebelled against the chaos sown by Istu. War raged that wracked the cosmos.

Istu fell.

Not even Felarod commanded power to unmake Istu, however. He had bound the demon with chains of spells in the depths of the Sky City and drawn a curtain of eternal sleep across its brain. The most furious efforts of the Dark Ones could not free their spawn. Perhaps in another turning of the galaxy the time would be right for Istu to gain freedom again, as perhaps it would be right for the demon's final destruction. The Dark Ones settled back to bide their time and nurse implacable hatred.

Istu knew none of this. Istu knew only dreams. Dreams of bitterness, of longing for revenge. But occasionally his slumber had been enlivened with strange stirrings and fresh sensations, the sense of venturing once again into the world, of slaking his thirst on pale, soft-skinned victims. Those times were good. Yet in time those ceased as well. No more did the demon's sleeping self hear the chanted summons from far above.

Not for five thousand years.

And then a voice began to tickle the underbelly of the sleeper's mind, drawing part of it out of itself and upward, ever upward. Istu resisted for a moment. Then memories of dark delight poured into his eternal dream. With a growing sense of anticipation, the sleeper responded to the call. . . .

Slits of yellow hellfire blazed beneath shelflike brows of stone. A tremor ran through its black form. It lifted a hand, stared at it, and then raised both arms above its head to cast a wordless shout of triumph and defiance toward the clouds above. No sound emerged from the being's mouth, but the roar reverberated in Moriana's mind and drove her close to madness.

The Vicar's yellow eyes swept down and fell upon the recumbent form of its sacrificial bride. The statue's lips spread. A forked tongue flickered over fist-sized teeth. The member between its legs rose like a charmed serpent.

Stone groaned and broke as it lifted one leg free of its pedestal. The other leg followed. A ponderous step sent vibrations through the marble pressed against Moriana's naked flesh. Four-fingered hands reached for her as the Vicar approached. She saw the blunted ram of its maleness lift toward her and felt the unyielding pressure, the tearing awful pain of entrance into her body. A voice that was hers and yet not hers screamed.

Red agony exploded into blackness.

"Wine," the vendor shouted, his lungs carrying his cry over the rumble of the mob. "Refresh your palates, honored ones, while you watch the traitor meet her fate. Twenty sipans the half-pint, wine!"

A stout, balding merchant with a teenaged, pock-marked mistress simpering at his elbow bought a pair of purple glass bottles. Fost accepted a handful of small silver oblongs, bobbed his head as if in gratitude, and limped away through the crowd. Slowly he edged toward the altar.

He played the role of a lamed bodyguard earning his keep by hawking his master's wine at the great event. His sword was strapped like a splint to his left leg, and both armed him and augmented his disguise. At the bottom of his leather pouch of bottles rested a round Athalar spirit jug and its volatile cargo.

"Wine!" The disguise worked well, at any rate. No one spared him a second glance. He felt the tingle of lust in the air as the crowd awaited Moriana's denudation.

Despite the day's chill, he sweated vigorously. *This has to be the most crack-brained scheme I've ever heard of,* he thought, not for the first time that day. The fact that he was the author of it from beginning to end didn't comfort him at all.

"Ahhhh!" A sigh rippled through the mob as a Monitor stripped away Moriana's cloak. Fost's heart jumped within his chest. Again he felt the urge to rip loose his sword and lunge to the rescue, as he had wanted to do when he'd entered the Circle and first saw her marching the slow march of the condemned. A glance at the massed ranks of soldiers on the ground between him and the princess, and the squadrons of eagles wheeling overhead, stifled the urge at once. *Lovely wench,* he allowed himself to think. *What a waste if this doesn't succeed.*

A tug at his sleeve brought him 'round to produce two bottles for a lean aristocrat with a jewel in one nostril. The pomaded dandies and the looks they exchanged reminded Fost of High Medurim.

His eyes scanned the crowd. Mingling with the onlookers would be Uriath's men, carrying jugs like the one in his pouch. That part of the original plan remained, to use the fire elementals to draw attention from the altar. At first it had seemed a cold-blooded scheme even to Fost, but the eagerness with which the mob anticipated Moriana's doom robbed him of any compassion for them.

He caught sight of a tow-headed figure making his way through the crush of bodies. In a drab workman's smock, Erlund walked with legs bent under his burden, a pitch-pot resting on a brazier of coals, with handles to insulate his hands and a leather apron protecting his belly. There wasn't a good reason for a worker to be abroad in the Circle with a pot of hot pitch, but nowhere in Fost's experience were folk inclined to question a common laborer who was obviously going about his business. These people didn't disappoint him. They edged away from the heat and stench of the pitch-pot, but otherwise paid Erlund no heed.

Fost stood near the ranks of soldiers holding back the crowd. A sudden crunching noise grabbed his attention. He looked over the soldiers' heads and gasped. The statue had uprooted itself and strode toward the captive princess.

The nearness of such magic overwhelmed him. For a mad moment all he could think of was flight. Anywhere, anyhow—even straight over the lip of the Well, if this would get him away from the demon.

His instinct for survival saved him from panic. Any Medurimite street urchin knew instinctively when he'd attracted the attention of the authorities. A prickling along his spine warned him something was amiss. He jerked himself into control and back to the problem he faced.

An officer eyed him suspiciously. Gaping at the statue come to life was not unusual. But something in Fost's manner had alerted the man. He gimped forward, dragging his stiff leg.

"I grow weary of my burden, lordly one," he said to the man, dropping his eyes in the deference proper for ground-born when addressing a child of the Sky City. "Would the colonel and his gallant men partake of my wine, as a gift from my humble self?"

The officer, who was plainly no more than a lieutenant of infantry, grinned acceptance. The last of the squat bottles were dispensed to the troopers. Caught up in the mood of the event, they forgot discipline to the extent of prying open the seals with daggers or simply breaking off the necks on the pavement. Purple wine gurgled down throats and slopped onto black tunics. Fost bobbed his head at them, smiling servilely. Then he saw what the idol was doing and the smile hardened on his lips.

Delight surged through the living stone of the demon's Vicar. Yet sensations lost for millenia awoke only part of the sleeping demon's mind. They stirred an elemental and primitive part, capable of tasting raw sensation and feeling raw emotion. That tiny fragment of the intellect responding to a bribe of carnal pleasure was enough to make the ruler who invoked it the mightiest sorceror of the Sundered Realm.

Howling like a maddened beast, Erlund threw himself through the crowd. He jostled soldiers aside. One shrieked and fell down flapping as pitch splashed onto his tunic and ignited. Alone on the cleared area of the Circle immediately behind the Vicar, Erlund dropped the brazier and flung the steaming pitch onto the broad back of the statue.

The horrid rhythm of the basalt hips never faltered. As the squad stared at the Vicar, Fost lunged a hand into his pouch and cast the spirit jug at the idol. The pot bounced off a churning dark shoulder and fell to the marble flagging, shattered.

The salamander flashed free. It was a small one, a green shimmer against the day's grayness. For a moment it hung in the air. Then it sensed the fumes, volatile and seductive. It moved.

One instant the Vicar reveled in single-minded joy as it raped the bound woman. The next the sun fell through the clouds and lit upon its back. The violence of its mental shout of pain blasted through the city.

Normal fire would not even have drawn its attention. But the fire of the salamander ate greedily at the clinging pitch and turned the stone molten where it touched. The demon Istu was in no danger; it slept far beneath the streets, as invulnerable as it was immobile. But the spark of its life which animated the Vicar knew dreadful agony. It wheeled, saw a pitiful man-thing crouching at its back, and stared at him. It reached down, caught up the creature by its leather covering, and began to rip off its limbs, like a small boy dismembering a flying insect.

A fresh blaze of agony brought Moriana awake. She no longer felt the piercing pain in her loins. Only a throbbing ache remained. The crowd sounds that washed against her ears had changed from lewdness to terror. Nearby, someone screamed.

A jerk at her right wrist made her open her eyes.

"Just lie still," Fost said, "and I'll have you free in a second." As she lay unbelieving, he quickly cut through the bonds that held her other hand and feet.

"What . . ." she began.

Fost grabbed her waist and flung himself backwards. The hard pavement bruised Moriana's limbs as he rolled atop her. A streak of light flared viciously overhead with a hiss and sizzle as a deathbolt from Synalon drew a charred line across the altar. The sorceress shrieked her fury and prepared another lightning-cast.

The blue flash caught the Vicar's attention. Its pseudo-awareness identified magic fire and the one who cast it with the cause of its pain. It turned, casually tossing the armless, legless husk that had been Erlund into the Well. The stink of fire-magic hung like a fog around the tall woman in white. It went for her, arms outstretched to maim and hurt and kill.

A bird rider swooped on Fost as he dragged Moriana to her feet. The Guardsman misjudged his distance and passed too close to the blazing statue. Eagle and rider erupted in a ball of green flame.

Moriana stood, still babbling questions. Fost looked around frantically. The rescue had gone off as planned —but where was his diversion? No other fire elementals frolicked among the spectators. The crowd had thinned considerably, but the ranks of soldiers Fost had burst through to reach the altar stood with backs unthreatened. All had their pikes leveled. Uriath's promised support hadn't materialized. Fost and Moriana were caught between the anvil of the troops and the hammer-like fists of the raging statue.

Only one course lay open. Gripping Moriana's wrist, Fost turned, took three running steps, and vaulted over the altar straight at Synalon. The black-haired princess gaped at him, hair flying as she swiveled her head from him to the advancing statue and back. Moriana managed to scramble over the still-smoking altar as her sister dropped flat to avoid a roundhouse sweep of the courier's broadsword. The soldiers on that side of the altar had fled the onslaught of the Vicar, leaving their mistress as thoroughly in danger as Fost's allies had left him. Hard on Fost's heels Moriana followed, joining the shrieking tide of humanity streaming away from the demon's wrath. In an instant they were across the Circle and into the safety of the city's twisting streets.

Synalon struggled to rise before the Vicar tore her asunder, as it had killed Erlund. Her plan lay in ruins. She had meant to beguile the demon with pleasure; she had given it searing anguish. Istu would not forget. Despairing, she considered letting the statue wreak its vengeance on her.

But she was no less a princess of the city than her sister. She straightened, a slim, slight figure before the monster's bulk. Her lips shaped the words of dismissal.

And then she realized it was too late.

Wings boomed over her head. A wiry shape dropped to the marble. In astonishment, the Vicar stopped to gaze at this puny thing that dared interpose itself with its pathetic sword and javelin. Doomed but unflinching, Prince Rann Etuul faced the maddened Vicar.

At the end of a street radiating from the Circle of the Skywell, Fost paused to let Moriana catch up. Her hair hung in strings about her face and thin rivulets of blood ran down her thighs, but she seemed in good enough condition. Looking past her, Fost saw Terror fall from the sky to drop Rann between the statue and his cousin. Synalon's voice reached Fost as she shrilled a chant. A vast black arm lashed out and swept Rann like a doll from the Vicar's path.

Moriana's hand sought Fost's. He picked her up in his arms and ran.

* * *

Later, sheltered against a building in the palace district, Fost stopped, gasping for breath. When it no longer felt as if spears pierced his lungs each time he breathed, he turned to Moriana.

"I owe you my life and soul," she whispered, "and no Etuul shirks her debts. That which you seek is in the penthouse of the northwestern tower of the palace. It's doubtless guarded by sorcery, but I think you can seize the philosopher's jug." She dropped her eyes. "Words are too small for thanks. Farewell."

Fost spent several breaths eyeing her appreciatively. For all her ordeals of the past few days, she was still breathtakingly lovely. In her disheveled nakedness, she stood as proud as any queen could hope to.

"Don't talk nonsense, wench," he told her. He took off his peddler's cloak and wrapped it around her shoulders. "Come along. We'd best reach the palace before the Guard collects its wits!"

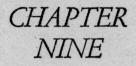

CHAPTER NINE

Blue lightnings surrounded Synalon's head in a crackling nimbus as she surveyed the wreckage of her sitting chamber. A mage lay spreadeagled on the floor, his chest blasted open by a deathbolt. The wounds that had claimed the lives of three palace guards were obviously of more mundane origin.

"How did he get here?" she screamed. "The spirit said Moriana robbed him in the night and got away. How did that dirt-spawned dog reach the city?"

A Monitor officer and several magicians stood clumped in the doorway. The officer cleared his throat. "We assumed that the Princess Moriana hijacked the balloon and killed its crew; it seemed so apparent that was the way she'd gained access to the city that we never troubled to question the ghost about it." He paled at the look in Synalon's eye, swallowed hard, and continued. "Now we feel she placed the crewmen under a spell of compulsion, and the barbarian, lacking her knowledge of either sorcery or aeronautics, resorted to force to reach the city."

"You *assumed*." Contempt filled the words. "Your assumption has cost us dearly, Gulaj." The man cringed. Synalon turned the full heat of her displeasure on the trio of sorcerors. Their shaven heads bobbed up and down. Fearful perspiration had begun to make the cabalistic designs painted on their skulls run down their cheeks. "And how fares my gracious cousin?"

The eldest mage looked at the next eldest, who

pivoted his head to peer expectantly at the youngest. That worthy only just saved himself from looking around for someone else with whom to saddle the unhappy task of answering.

"H-he fares well, O Mistress of the Clouds. His ribs are cracked where the Vicar struck him. He sleeps well under sedation; a few days of rest shall make him whole again."

Synalon paced to her beryl throne and sat. The silk cushion lay askew. She paid it as little heed as she did the remnants of her headdress hanging in her face or the pink-tipped breast that peeked from her torn pearl-white robe. Rann had bought her time to conjure the life out of the Vicar and return it to Itsu, but the stony fingers had been clutching at her garments when the light went out of the statue's eyes. Dispatching the elemental had taken little more than a gesture. But the struggle with the Vicar had brought her near exhaustion.

"He shall not have days to rest," Synalon said. "Go and rouse him. Even now the Guards comb the sky for the fugitives, but I expect the prince will have ample opportunity to redeem his failure by personally bringing the criminals to justice." After a moment's hesitation, the mages turned and left.

Gulaj started to follow them.

"Colonel." Synalon's soft voice brought him to a halt just inside the doorway, which was blocked by the massive ironbound door, blasted off its hinges by Moriana's sorcery. "Did you hear me give you leave to go?"

"Your pardon, Lady. Istu . . ."

A lance of fire from a pointing fingertip cut him off. Blue-white light filled the chamber. The colonel fell forward in a reek of burnt flesh and ozone.

Synalon paid the corpse no mind. It was Rann who

deserved to die. But Rann she could not spare. Only the prince, she was sure, had the skill necessary to recover Erimenes and work retribution on those who had stolen him away.

Why did he help her, that miserable groundling of a courier? She robbed him! Sparks popped from her fingertips as fury gripped her. The injustice tied her muscles into knots of frenzied anger. She sat for a hundred heartbeats, clenched and sweating at the deviousness of her twin sister.

The fit passed. She slumped limply in the chair. A shaft of sunlight fell through clouds to waken the green fire in the gemstone arm of her throne. Moodily, she drew herself up and stared out the window at her bird riders wheeling their mounts about the sky.

"My thanks for saving me from those despicable rogues," Erimenes said.

"You dare speak of roguery?" Moriana shouted. "You, who begged to be allowed to witness my torture?"

"I toyed with them, no more," Erimenes said airily. "If I seemed sufficiently intent on watching them torment you, I knew they'd never touch you. Psychology, you see. It must have worked. Your flawless skin remains intact."

Moriana's eyes smoldered. "They tortured my friends to death before me. I'd rather they'd worked their fiendishness on my body." She snatched at the jar once more suspended in its pouch slung beneath Fost's arm. The courier fended her warily. "Psychology, you say! Is that what you call it, to sit talking of exotic perversions with Synalon while my loved ones died, screaming for oblivion?"

"I was only trying to win her confidence," said Erimenes. "And I knew those ward spells she'd cast hindered your powers. Rann felt nothing, lacking in any magical skills, and could have physically over-whelmed you. And Synalon, well, she was scarcely in the position of having to use magic while you were chained. So, you see, my behavior was consistent and in your best interests. In fact, I . . ."

"Enough!" Fost bellowed before Moriana could re-ply. "For Gormanka's sake, you'll alert the entire dis-trict." His voice reverberated the length of the street and sent foraging rats scurrying for cover.

"Here," he said in a softer tone, unslinging the pouch and handing it to Moriana. "Hold onto this blatherer. I'm supposed to meet my contact with the underground, if they haven't botched that as well." He glimpsed the glow in Moriana's eyes. "Don't throw him over the edge. It's not likely to do him much harm."

"Of course not," Erimenes declared. "Being im-material, a fall of a thousand feet would be as a . . ." A vicious shake by the princess shut him up in mid-sentence.

Leaving Moriana to deal with the dead philosopher, Fost moved up the block, around the corner and slipped into an alley. After the rescue, he was to bring Moriana to a certain warehouse near the docks at the edge of the city. He had been told the route to take. He didn't go that way now. Instead he traced a round-about course, to bring him upon his contact from an unexpected direction. He'd had enough of Uriath's lack of security.

He had no difficulty in sneaking up behind the undergrounder. Fost was in his element now, far more than the dilettantes of the resistance. He paused a mo-ment to make sure that the contact was alone. Then he moved, as swift and silent as light.

A heavy hand muffled the cry that broke from Luranni's lips as a dagger-tip pricked her throat. "So you came," he said. "Was it mere oversight that I was left facing the city's whole army alone?" She shook her head, her eyes glazing with fear.

"Make a noise louder than a whisper and I'll slit your throat," Fost said before taking his hand away from her mouth.

"No treachery," she breathed. "I swear it! I don't know what went wrong. The men with the elementals said they never got the word to act."

The courier hesitated, still holding the girl immobile, his dagger hovering near her neck. The cinnamon scent and the nearness of her body awoke memories, but they had grown pallid and distant. Finally he shrugged and let her go. Her tale was likely true. He could expect no more from the amateurs in the underground than he had already gotten.

"I suppose you've come to tell me your people failed to find us a way to get to the surface."

She shook her head, sending a soft cascade of brown hair swirling out around her shoulders. "No." Her eyes were bigger and rounder than normal and the word came hesitantly. She obviously thought that the man she had taken to bed a few days earlier was ready to slay her at any moment. "The way is prepared. But it'll be hazardous. Won't you stay? With me?"

"No. Synalon's men will take this town apart clear to Istu's bedchamber on the chance that we'll remain." He looked into her eyes. Emotions stirred within him. Her invitation hadn't fallen on deaf ears, and however ill her comrades had done by him, she had tried her best on his behalf. She'd come to mean something to him, as well. He couldn't leave without some explanation.

"Moriana and I have something we must do. If we succeed, our chances of freeing the city will be much improved. I can't say any more." He knew that Moriana's purpose in seeking the Amulet of Living Flame

opposed his own, though the reckoning of who should
have it had been put off for the moment.

"You have the parcel that you wanted?" she asked.
He nodded. "And you will deliver it as you intended?"

He hesitated. "Yes."

The faint cry of a circling war-bird drifted down
from the sky. Luranni gripped his arm. "We must
hurry," she said. He led her back to where Moriana
waited, hoping he didn't disengage his hand from hers
too blatantly.

"What have we here?" The words made Fost stop
and turn. Moriana stepped from a recessed doorway.
Her parted cloak revealed swatches of pale skin. Fost
grinned in appreciation. Here was no clumsy amateur.
She was almost as skilled as the courier himself.

"Yes, what have we?" Erimenes asked with interest.
"A lovely lass to be sure. Quite lively in bed, too, I
don't doubt."

Luranni gaped at the satchel, her expression turning
quickly to keen interest. Fost ground his teeth. She was
no more a fool than her father, except at the game of
insurrection. He knew she was quite capable of drawing conclusions he didn't wish made.

"Time to go," he urged, looking uneasily at the sky.

"You've not introduced us, dear Fost," Moriana
said, hanging back.

Fost groaned. The look that passed between the two,
emerald eyes to golden, left no room for secrets.

"This is Luranni, daughter of High Councillor Uriath.
Luranni, uh, meet the Princess Moriana."

"You could fight over him," Erimenes suggested
helpfully.

"We may as well give ourselves up as stand here any
longer," Fost said. Luranni gave him a narrow glance
and turned to lead the way.

Moriana let her get a few paces ahead before she asked, "What does this one mean to you?"

"A way out of this wretched city, nothing more."

Moriana scrutinized him like a bird sizing up possible prey, then followed the brown-haired girl.

"Faugh! It smells like bird droppings in here. Can't we seek out more wholesome surroundings?" Erimenes's voice rang with loftly disdain.

"If he suggests a trip to a brothel I'll use his jug for a chamber pot," said Fost. A strangled sound emerged from the jug. Fost peered around the darkened passageway. Luranni led the way, holding aloft a crystal vial shaped like a dove, which cast a heatless illumination like that of the lightfool. "But he's right. I do smell birds."

Moriana sniffed the air. "No common birds," she said. They rounded a bend in the tunnel. Sunlight fell through a barred aperture and splashed the floor and walls of a chamber cut from the skystone of the City's base. "It's the scent of war-birds. Luranni, where are we?"

"An ancient aerie, last used during the wars with the surface-dwellers. My family has known about it for generations; our cargo balloons moor near here."

"Why do we waste time here, then?" asked Erimenes. "Surely we've better uses for our time than a survey of historic sites. Of what interest is this abandoned . . ."

A rustling noise came from the shadowed recesses of the aerie. Fost's sword hissed free of its bird-leather scabbard.

"Abandoned?" he said quietly. "I don't think so."

A figure appeared, dim and monstrous in the gloom. Higher than Fost's head it loomed, approaching with a lurching waddle. The hefty broadsword felt as inadequate as a lady's poniard in the courier's hand.

"What kind of trap is this?" he hissed at Luranni, as he made ready to launch himself at the monstrosity.

"Wait!" Her cloak flapping behind her, Moriana lunged at the creature. Fost shouted a warning. The cry died on his lips as the princess threw her arms about the giant shape and hugged it fiercely. "Ayoka!" she cried. "Oh, Ayoka, they told me you were dead!"

Standing in the light, Fost saw a war-eagle of the Sky City, huge and deep of chest, its razor-sharp beak immense. But white cataracts crusted the saucer-shaped eyes, and the once-sleek body shed feathers in a constant molt. The bird was obviously an ancient creature, with few days left him.

"He came to us here, the night Derora died," said Luranni, standing at the courier's side. The big man was acutely aware of the soft hip pressing into his. "A watchman heard noises and found him. The eagles lack man-speech, unlike the slit-tongued ravens Synalon favors, and none of us know the war-birds' tongue. I recognized him as Princess Moriana's mount, though, so we fed and watered him, and closed the gate to keep him safe from aerial patrols. My father says he's sound enough to bear you to the ground."

Fost eyed the creature dubiously. Ayoka had once been a mighty bird indeed. That much was clear. But his prime had long since passed. And for even a young bird to bear the combined weight of Fost and Moriana would be a considerable task. Fost sheathed his sword and shook his head skeptically.

Moriana knelt on the ground, stroking the ragged feathers and sobbing, crooning to the bird in an unfamiliar language. The bird preened her long blonde hair with his beak and made some burbling reply.

"He says that the night the queen died, a palace functionary named Kralfi came to warn him to flee," said Erimenes. " 'Fly, O winged warrior; we human friends of the princess and true queen are lost, but still may you serve bright Moriana.' Very poetic, if you go in for that sort of sticky sentimentality. Not to my taste at all. Give me a bawdy limerick any day. Have you heard this one? 'There was a maid of Me-durim . . .' "

Fost ignored the spirit. "Is that actually what he said?" Moriana turned a tearful face to him and nodded. "Can he carry both of us?" The princess spoke to the bird. The eagle threw back its head and voiced a cry that filled the chamber like a trumpet blast. For all the bird's decrepitude, there was no denying the power in his call.

"He says he can," Moriana declared, standing. "And I believe him." She turned to Luranni and asked, "Do you have a saddle for him?"

The girl nodded and disappeared into the shadows. She came back dragging a pile of tack and other equipment. Fost stood idly by, fretting at his inability to be of any use, as Moriana selected a double harness and cinched it to Ayoka's back. From the stack of gear, she drew two short recurved bows and two filled quivers.

"No, thank you," Fost said as she offered him one. "I couldn't hit the Dowager Empress in the rump at three paces with one of those. A sword is more to my liking."

"A pity," Moriana said with a grimace. "There's little call for swordplay in bird-back combat." She hoisted herself agilely into the front of the double-seated saddle and threw her legs forward around the eagle's neck. "Here, climb up behind and strap yourself in. This is a training saddle. You're not likely to fall out of it."

Gingerly, Fost clambered up onto Ayoka's broad back. The bird grunted at his weight. He winced and fixed a sturdy strap around his middle.

"How about you?" he asked Moriana.

"I was born to the back of an eagle," she replied haughtily. "I need nothing to hold me in the saddle. Nor would I ever use a strap. I need my freedom if we're to make it past the patrols."

Fost blinked. It hadn't occurred to him they might have to fight their way to the surface. The ride down would be harrowing enough without being beset by swarms of bird-riding Guardsmen. He fixed Erimenes's satchel to the harness and loosened his sword in its scabbard, just in case.

Luranni unlatched the circular gate and threw it wide. "Farewell, my Princess," she said to Moriana. The bird walked forward, stooped under his double burden. Luranni stood on tiptoe, grabbed Fost and dragged him down for an impassioned kiss. "And you, my courier," she said, eyes shining brightly.

"Our thanks, Luranni, daughter of Uriath," said Moriana. To Fost's surprise she sounded sincere. "When we return, we shall bring with us the freedom of the city!" She nudged Ayoka. The bird reeled forward and pitched headlong into space.

Fost shouted in dismay as the prairie hurtled up at them. It seemed he had left his stomach behind in the aerie. Nausea and terror fought for control of his senses.

Huge wings burst from Ayoka's sides. Their headlong plummet shallowed into a wide, circling dive. Fost clung to handfuls of feathers, only slowly realizing that their descent was controlled.

Moriana's cloak billowed in his face. He brushed it aside, allowing it to stream over his shoulder. He was rewarded with the sight of her slim, white back and shapely buttocks flattened against the high-cantled saddle. He had forgotten that the Sky City's fugitive princess was still naked beneath the borrowed cloak.

"What a vision of loveliness!" Erimenes caroled. "Doesn't it stir your manhood, Fost? Why, if the delectable princess were to lean a touch farther forward, perhaps you could plunge your doubtlessly raging manhood—"

Fost thumped the jar. Hard.

Still, he thought, *is it such a bad idea? Moriana does stir my manhood.* The thought of making love a thousand feet in the air on the back of an eagle had a definite appeal. Fost was considering leaning forward to suggest it to Moriana when the princess turned her head and looked straight past him.

"Hold tight," she ordered. A hand reached behind her for one of the quivers slung across her back.

Fost's head snapped around. A trio of winged shapes drifted down toward them from the rim of the city. He thought he saw a flash of a pale face and arm as Luranni waved from the aerie. Then the gate slammed shut as the girl fell back to avoid drawing the attention of the bird riders who pursued Ayoka.

A raucous cry reached their ears. More birds appeared until half a dozen Guardsmen were swooping down on the fleeing pair. Fost felt his stomach tie itself into a knot.

"A fight! Glorious!" Erimenes was plainly beside himself with glee. "Oh, what a memorable battle this shall be!"

"I hope I'm alive to remember it," Fost said sourly. With morbid fascination, he kept his head craned around to watch the pursuers approach. The nearer three were armed with javelins and bows. One held a long lance, its head designed to break away from the shaft when it struck, so that it wouldn't drag its wielder to his doom. The Guards wore no armor. They depended on the speed and maneuverability of their mounts for protection. And in both those respects, their birds would hold every advantage over a half-senile eagle who bore three times the weight they did.

Something whined past Fost's ear. The rider on the left dropped his bow and tumbled from his saddle. Silently he spun groundward, arms and legs splayed.

"Marvelously shot!" Erimenes cried. "As lovely a sight as your own naked limbs, Princess."

Fost didn't think so. He knew it had been the bird rider's intention to slay him and Moriana, or return them to captivity and torture beyond imagining. Fost had often reveled in the hot rush of a foeman's blood as his blade bit deep, but the lonely suddenness of death in the air bothered him. Nor was he insensible that the bird rider's fate could be his.

The tactician in Fost appraised the peril they faced. He had no experience in aerial warfare, but it was plain to see that with their advantage in height, the pursuers could fall on their quarry whenever they chose. Moriana's arrows might claim more of them. On the other hand, some of their opponents were armed with bows, too.

Fost drew his sword. Moriana cast him an unreadable glance over her shoulder but said nothing. It might do him no good; still, the feel of the leather-wrapped hilt in his fist comforted him.

The world suddenly spun through a quarter circle. A pressure of Moriana's knees had sent the giant war-bird wheeling to one side to avoid the onslaught of the two nearest Guardsdmen. A high wailing cry broke from a feathered throat as an arrow buried itself to the fletching in an eagle's chest. The Guard shrieked as his lifeless mount began the last long fall.

But there was no eluding his comrade. The gray-plumed war-bird had flattened its wings to its sides. Its rider lay along its neck, lance couched and aimed for the kill.

Sunlight gleamed on the keen lance head. Moriana strove frantically to nock another arrow. Erimenes gibbered orgiastically in the fulfillment of blood. Neither could change the grim judgment of the steel arrowing at Fost's heart.

His senses dilated until all that existed was the lance point, glittering and hungering for flesh. Fury exploded within him. Bellowing, he swung his sword with all his strength.

The blade bit. The lance head went cartwheeling away, its tip laying open his cheek in passing. The blunted lance struck him full in the chest.

Breath burst from his body. Blackness and vivid stars whirled around his eyes. Instinctively his hand grabbed, felt smooth hardness, closed. An awful wrench sent agony stabbing from his abused shoulder, and he was thrown violently against the restraining strap around his middle.

A howling beat through the haze of agony and breathlessness that wrapped his brain. Colossal wingtips brushed his face. The war-bird rushed by, riderless. The man who'd sat astride its back a moment before was falling after his two comrades, unseated by the reflex that had made Fost grip the haft of his lance as it struck.

Moriana's head turned. Her lips formed words twisted by the rush of the wind.

"What?" Fost shouted. His voice sounded rusty and as hoarse as if he had been inhaling smoke.

"Are you all right?" she cried. He felt his chest gingerly before nodding his head. He felt as though he'd been hit on the breastbone with a sledgehammer.

"Struck with your typical lack of chivalry," said Erimenes sourly. "Not one drop of blood did I see spilled."

"That's not true," Fost said, touching his torn cheek.

An arrow whirred by not a hand's-breadth from his head. He yelped and twisted in the saddle to look behind, as Moriana drew her bow to return fire.

One of the three remaining pursuers had forged ahead of the rest. His mount squalled battle lust not a hundred feet behind the tip of Ayoka's tailfeathers. Even as Fost watched, the great bird-shape swelled. Moriana shot. Her arrow went wide. The eagle was too close for another shot. She slung her bow and gave all her thought to flying.

Voicing his own harsh battle-cry, Ayoka sideslipped, evading another shot from the Guardsman's bow. Still the archer's mount closed with its prey. Ayoka was laboring now. His breath came in vast, heaving wheezes, and Fost could feel the bird's heart hammering between his thighs. Moriana threw him into defensive turns, first to the right, then to the left. Ayoka's size, immense even for a war-bird, served him poorly now. The smaller eagle behind matched his every maneuver effortlessly, coming nearer and nearer.

The Guardsman held an arrow to his cheek. Fost saw the excitement and triumph glowing from the man's dark, thin features. The courier guessed he was holding fire, hoping to cripple Ayoka and force him down. The reward would be great for presenting Synalon with the corpses of her sister and the outlander who had thwarted her; a thousand times greater would be the reward for whoever presented her with their living bodies.

The wind of the attacking eagle's wings pounded Fost. Their sound grew louder as the thump of Ayoka's pinions ceased. A command from Moriana had made him press wings to his sides for a last, desperate dive. It was a futile ploy. The pursuing bird folded its own wings, swooping for the kill.

Fost shook his sword in the Guardsman's grinning
face, shouting defiance even as he steeled himself for
Hell Call. With a sound like stone striking stone,
Ayoka's wings broke from his flanks and seized the
air. The giant bird slammed to a stop in mid-dive.
Fost's defiance turned to astonishment before he went
face-first into Ayoka's feathers.

The pursuing soldier acted too late. His mount
threw out its wings in a braking maneuver, but its speed
was too great and the span of its pinions too small.
The eagle slid beneath Ayoka and stalled. Moriana's
bow sang. The Guardsman uttered a choking yell as
the broadhead arrow bit through his chest and pinned
him to his mount.

Ayoka gave a cry that was half a gasp of pain. Fost
snapped his head around to see a javelin sticking
through the bird's right wing. Bravely, Ayoka flapped
on but he now flew in a tight spiral. Only by some
miracle did he keep from giving in to the anguish that
filled him. As it was, the dart transfixing his wing
interfered with its motion. All he could do was circle
down and down.

Shouting hoarse exultation, the bird riders orbited
him. The ancient bird had put up an epic fight, but
with the dart through his wing he couldn't maneuver
properly. The kill had become a certainty.

Moriana loosed arrows as fast as she could, scarcely
aiming, to keep their foes at bay.

"Out!" she shouted at Fost. "You must pull it out,
or we fall."

He started to protest. Undoing his safety strap at
this moment seemed suicidal. And the kind of gym-
nastics it would take to pull the javelin out of Ayoka's
wing . . . he felt dizzy at the very thought.

"Ah, such a fight," Erimenes sighed. "Too bad that

it must end so soon. I'll almost sorrow to see your lifesblood shed, friend Fost. But what must be, must be."

That did it.

"You've seen all my blood you're going to today, demon in a jug," the courier growled. Not permitting himself to think, he unfastened the strap that held him in his saddle, sheathed his sword and turned to crawl out along the weakly pumping wing.

Understanding what the man was doing, Ayoka stopped flapping and held his wings straight for a glide. He sensed no updrafts on which to kite. They kept corkscrewing inexorably downward, faster now that his wing-beating had ceased resisting gravity.

The bird's body canted as Fost's weight shifted off-center. Fost clutched the wing, felt the hardness of bone and muscle and probed for the javelin. A glimpse of the ground spinning madly below sent cold fire dancing along his nerves. He shut his eyes and groped.

His fingertips bumped wood. He gripped the javelin's shaft and tugged hard. Ayoka coughed. The eagle's body jerked in response to the pain. Somehow, Fost had gotten tangled with the saddle harness. His body swung momentarily free of the sail-sized pinion, held only by his entangled foot.

"Gormanka!" he grunted, wishing the deity actually could aid him.

Realizing that intervention of a divine power wasn't likely, and that he must rely on his own abilities, Fost reached back and drew his sword. Moriana's harassing fire kept the Guardsmen at a distance, but she had to shoot too rapidly for accuracy. As usual, Erimenes was cheering both sides of the fray impartially.

Fost lunged forward and caught the javelin. He began to hack at its shaft just above the barbed head, trying to keep from jarring it in the wound. He felt the tremors of agony shudder through the mighty wing-muscles.

"Hurry," came Moriana's voice. "He cannot hold on much longer!"

The barb came away. A heave threw Fost backward, pulling the javelin out of Ayoka's wing with the same motion that sent the courier sprawling across the eagle's back. Ayoka swung away to the left. Fost would have fallen, but Moriana turned to grab him. Then Ayoka's wings were beating again. Their headlong plummet eased.

Frustrated, the Guardsmen charged. With a jarring impact, Ayoka twisted to meet one. Fost managed to grab a convenient strap with his sword hand and almost dropped his weapon. He smelled new rankness. A shadow fell on him. He jerked himself against Ayoka, his cheek pressing into Moriana's bare rump. Talons like heated wires raked his back.

Cursing, he flung the beheaded javelin after the eagle that had clawed him. The spinning shaft struck its tail and knocked free a handful of its stabilizing feathers. The bird pitched forward, righted itself with a wild plunging of its wings, and went fluttering away, fighting to stay airborne as its rider clung helplessly to its back.

Fost heard screaming. Ayoka had plucked the other Guard from his saddle and now held him in his claws while his beak ripped and tore flesh. A few savage strokes caused the man to hang limp and blood-soaked. Contemptuously, Ayoka let the body drop.

"A splendid battle. There was nearly enough blood spilled to satisfy me," Erimenes said. "Still, there's the matter of one surviving bird rider. Hadn't we best pursue him and finish him off?"

Miles across the sky, Fost saw the outline of the disabled bird still struggling to stay aloft. "Break off," he said wearily. "We'd best not go looking for trouble; I'm sure we'll find ample quantities of it before we come to Athalau." He listened a moment to Ayoka's breathing. "Nor can this bird carry us forever."

Erimenes said something sulky. Moriana leaned forward, conversing with the bird in its warbling pidgin.

"He says he sees my riding dog. I ordered the beast to keep pace with the city as best he could. It's no great trick. The city moves slowly enough to leave him time to sleep and search for food." A puzzled frown creased her forehead. "He also sees several other dogs that seem to be pulling something. He can't be more specific. He doesn't have the concepts."

Fost laughed delightedly. "Never mind. That's my own team and sled. I told them to follow your beast, thinking you might have him pace the Sky City. They're good dogs. They know how to forage in harness." He smiled at her continued look of bewilderment. "They led me to you."

"But how? I covered my scent with minor spells."

"But not the scent of the gruel from Kest-i-Mond's ever-filled bowl." He explained to her the trick he'd used for tracking and found himself telling the whole story of his flight to the city and his adventure there— suitably edited.

"But one thing still bothers me," he finished. "Why do they call that ugly statue the Vicar of Istu? I thought a vicar was some old dodderer who kept the stocks of incense and sacramental wine in order."

"The word means *substitute* or *representative*," Moriana told him.

"Oh."

The ground flew by below. They came within the weaker human sight of the dogs. Moriana's long-legged mount loped along, with Fost's team dragging his sled on a parallel course some distance away.

With Ayoka gratefully winging his way to a landing, Moriana turned once more to look at Fost. The light in her eyes woke his blood. He put a hand on the nape of her neck and drew her face to his for a lingering kiss.

She screamed.

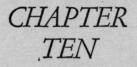

CHAPTER TEN

Fost jerked back. For a moment he wondered if he'd done something to draw such an outcry. She pointed past him into the sky.

Like smoke, a small black cloud swirled around the fringe of the great dark stone that was the city. As Fost and Moriana looked on, the blackness detached itself and began moving downwards. With a shock, Fost realized the cloud was heading for them.

"My sister dares not disperse the Guardsmen, lest rebellion break out while they hunt us," said Moriana. "Doubtless a company or two is being readied for the chase. In the meantime, she sets the ravens on our trail."

Fost frowned at the cloud. Ravens? The image leaped into his mind. The balloon that had brought him to the city, shorn of its gondola, had been slashed and ripped by a savage attack of the black ravens.

Luranni's voice echoed through his mind: *their talons are poisoned.*

He quickly took stock of their situation. He found little to lift the chill that had settled on his soul. A scant five arrows remained in Moriana's quiver. The bird they rode was exhausted. The dogs could never outrun the swift-winged black killers, and the prairie's grassy swells offered no concealment from the air.

"We may fail," Moriana said, seeing the bleakness in his eyes, "but for my part I'd rather die with venom in my blood than spend eternity writhing in Istu's grip. You've won me a decent death, warrior. My thanks for that."

Fost told himself that this was small recompense for the loss of immortality. Her words warmed him anyway.

Taloned feet touched ground. Ayoka took a few running steps on powerful legs as his wings fought the forward momentum. He came to a halt and sank to the grass. Moriana leaped from his back and ran toward her dog, who turned to meet her with a happy bark. Fost's dogs halted, their pointed ears pricking as they sensed their master's presence once again.

Moriana dug furiously in the pack she retrieved from her dog. "We'll make a fire. Perhaps we can stand them off with torches."

"For how long?" Fost asked. When he didn't get an answer, he bent to help her gather clumps of grass. The long strands were beginning to go dry and brittle with the onset of winter. At least starting a fire wouldn't be hard.

The ravens' shrill, evil cries reached them. Fost waited for Moriana to produce flint and steel. He jumped back when a word and a gesture brought the pile of grass into a blaze. It was easy to forget that the woman was a sorceress as well as a princess, thief, and warrior.

He took a handful of burning straw and stood. Already the swarm circled overhead, cackling gleefully among themselves, savoring the fear and consternation of their victims. Moriana stood by his side. She gripped his hand briefly. He returned the pressure without looking at her. His eyes were riveted on the great living cloud roiling above their heads.

A great ringing cry of anger rose from Ayoka's throat. He followed it. Like an immense projectile, he rose straight into the wheeling flock of ravens.

Black birds broke in all directions. Feathers flew and
dark shapes fell lifeless to the prairie. Ayoka had risen
to his final battle, and his foes had felt his wrath.

"Ayoka!" screamed Moriana. If he heard his mistress,
the war-bird gave no sign. His huge form was almost
totally obscured by shrieking ravens, but now and
again Fost caught the glint of a giant beak slashing.

Dead ravens fell like diseased rain. A straggler, or
one remembering his duty, dived on Fost and Moriana.
Fost swung his sword. The blade sheared through a
wing, causing the bird to drop flopping to the ground.
Moriana lopped off its head.

Fost looked into the sky. The late afternoon sun
dropped towards the Thails, casting a mellow golden
light over a scene of utter horror. Striking beaks had
burst Ayoka's eyes. Blood stained the white feathers
of his head and ran from a score of lesser wounds. But
even the poisons of the Sky City took time to kill a
creature as large as Ayoka. He was making each
second count.

His beak snapped and struck, shredding ravens like
old cloth. His talons clutched, closed on struggling
shapes until all movement stopped, and then dropped
the carcass to seize another. Even the eagle's wings
served him as weapons, buffeting the close-packed
ravens and dashing them to the ground, where Fost
and Moriana made short work of them.

With a shrilling of outrage and alarm, the ravens
broke away from the eagle. He traced a tight circle,
a wingtip smashing an incautious foe.

"Enchanted!" a raven croaked.

The survivors took up the panicked call: "He is
enchanted! We cannot harm him!"

Like a single frightened organism, the ravens spun
away and fled back up the sky toward home. Ayoka
floated serenely, turning his blinded eyes as if watch-

ing the rout of his attackers. His crimsoned beak
opened and a harsh cry rang across the prairie, defiant
and triumphant. Then his wings flowed upward like
quicksilver and his body dropped behind a low ridge.

Moriana started to run to him. Fost stopped her.
"He's dead. He gave his life to buy us time. Let's not
waste it." She fought him briefly, then slumped sobbing
against his chest.

He gave her a moment with her grief. Before he
moved to rouse her, she broke the embrace. "Let's go,"
she said, and her eyes were dry.

Her saddle and pack with her spare clothing and
gear lay miles behind. Fost introduced the princess to
his dogs, who took to her readily after giving their
master a noisy, face-licking greeting. The courier rummaged in his own sparse baggage, and in a short while
Moriana was decked out in rough breeches and a tunic
of homespun drab.

"I'll miss my sword," she said, ruefully eyeing the
few arrows remaining in her quivers.

After a few more seconds of searching, Fost found
a long, heavy-bladed knife, which Moriana thrust
through the length of rope she'd knotted around her
waist. Fost mounted the runners of his sled. Moriana
strode to her mount and swung astride it. The animal
whimpered and sidestepped nervously. She leaned low
and patted its neck, speaking softly to soothe it.

Not even Erimenes found much to say as they began
their long journey south.

"I freely acknowledge my failure, O Mistress of the
Clouds." Prince Rann sat before the beryl throne in
Synalon's disordered chamber, his head bowed. "I
implore you for the opportunity to redress my errors."

The mages hadn't needed to fetch the prince from

his sickbed. They had met him in the hallway, already clad in the purple and black of a bird rider. Despite the pain of cracked ribs hastily bound with linen bandages, the small man had walked erect to meet his royal cousin.

Now Synalon presented every appearance of a stern but just queen attempting to find the proper course to take with a trusted subordinate who'd proven derelict in his duties. It was all a sham, as Rann knew well. Synalon had already decided his fate. He knew that, too. He was still alive and free. Had the verdict gone against him, he would even now be straining his muscles against the inexorable pressure of his own rack. Or lying on the floor cindered and dead like the unfortunate Colonel Gulaj, whose body still sprawled near the door.

"I have decided," she said with a slow, regal nod. "In view of your past loyalty and service, you shall have the boon you crave. I charge you now to overtake and return to justice the traitor Moriana, her lowborn accomplice and, ah, whatever rightful property of the Crown the miscreants have stolen." She paused in thought while Rann hid a smile. "You may take a company of Guardsmen, no more. The city lies in grave danger of insurrection, thanks to the evil influences of my sister."

"I shall need no more, Your Majesty." His scars became a white net overlaying his features, as he thought of his own debts to settle with the fugitives. The coin was pain and humiliation. He would take payment in kind, a thousand-fold.

Synalon sat back in her throne. Dismissing the kneeling prince, she turned to the new palace chamberlain, who hovered anxiously at her elbow wringing fish-white hands.

"Tell me, Anacil," she said, "how long would it take to procure a hornbull?"

Southward and eastward fled the fugitives, on a line that would take them near the walls of Brev. Like all the cities of that Great Quincunx, Brev teemed with the paid agents of the Sky City. Fost and Moriana would forgo the pleasures of civilized accomodations for a night beneath the stars. They wouldn't thirst or hunger, though. Synalon had left the self-replenishing bowl and goblet Fost had taken from Kest-i-Mond's castle in the satchel with Erimenes's jug. The courier had given in to the spirit's whining pleas and taken out the resin pellets that jammed the bowl's lid open, so that Erimenes no longer had to ride sloshing about in gruel. Not at all to Fost's surprise, the philosopher displayed no gratitude.

Beyond the line of the Quincunx that connected Brev and Thailot, the prairie broke apart in a network of narrow ravines. Whether natural action of erosion had formed them, or as legend said, the very earth had cracked under the stresses of the War of Powers, couldn't be told. Some of the ravines ran with swift torrents of water birthed amid the snows and springs of the Thails. Others lay dry, with no sign of ever having carried streams. So much Fost learned from Moriana's descriptions. By now the sun poised fat and swollen, ready to burst itself on the jagged fangs of the mountains and spill daylight from the sky. Shadows masked the bottoms of the gorges, though from some issued the impatient murmur of running water. As they entered the cracked lands, the autumn-dried grasses of the prairie gave way to a short, coarse heather whose dark green and purple leaves masked prodigious thorns. They tinged the air with a faint, astringent odor. They also slowed down the pair considerably. The dagger-like thorns penetrated even the thick fur of Fost's dogs, forcing him and Moriana to pick their way around the densest growths.

Fost's mood began to lighten. He had faced over-whelming odds and won. He was on his way to adventure, with a woman at his side who possessed both beauty and skill in combat, and at the quest's end lay immortality. The fact that Moriana had ideas of her own about what should be done with the Amulet of Living Flame didn't trouble him now. The time to settle that issue was when it arose.

Now he rode beneath the open sky, and his nostrils gratefully drank in the freshness of the air. The medicinal aroma of the heather came as a relief after the intermingled scents of the Sky City. Thirty thousand years of habitation had imbued the city with a smell that was more an aura, never truly noticed after the first encounter, yet never absent and coloring every perception. It wasn't a bad odor, but Fost was glad to be free of it.

He looked back at the way they'd come and saw bands of glorious color staining the sky. With winter coming, the sun's arc had swung far to the north. Directly to the east, the Thail Mountains pulled tighter the cloaks of cold shadows, dotted only occasionally with towering, gold-tipped treetops. At the other end of the sky rose the green moon.

Fost studied the dark shapes moving slowly against the striations of orange and violet and indigo. Then, a dryness in his throat, he called out to Moriana to look. Her first glance confirmed his fears.

"War-birds," she said.

"At least ten bird riders against the two of you," said Erimenes thoughtfully, "and this time you're groundlings, and in the open. This promises to be interesting."

"Interesting it may well be," Moriana said, "but we won't meet them in the open. That would be suicide—and how much fun would that be to watch?"

For once, Erimenes lacked a reply. Signaling Fost to follow, Moriana rode toward the head of a cut that fell steeply to join the maze of canyons. Sword in hand, Fost steered his team in her wake. They hurtled through the heather, ignoring the thorns that raked them constantly.

Moriana braked to a sudden halt; Fost's sled slid to a stop behind her. She leaped from her mount and slapped the dog. With a yelp, it kept on running. She had her sword out and was hacking at his dogs' harnesses.

"What are you doing?" Fost demanded.

"This ravine's only a few feet wide . . . room only for us. Besides, the dogs might throw them off the scent. And we'll need a roof of some kind over our heads to keep us safe from aerial attacks."

Fost joined her in chopping down the squat, dry brush. "Why can't you use sorcery against the Guardsmen?"

"The same reason I didn't use magic to free myself back in the city. Synalon's ward-spells protect her from enchantment, and her Guardsmen almost as well. I can't even use a compulsion on them as I did with the guards at the balloon dock." She swept a lock of hair from her eyes. "There are limitations."

Five minutes work allowed them to bridge the narrow cut with the dense brush over a six-foot length. It was slim cover, but enough to keep off the birds and spoil their riders' aim, and, with the sun setting, the light would be gone in minutes.

Huddled beneath the thorny covert, they heard angry squawks from thwarted eagles. "Land, men," came a voice. "We'll take them afoot."

Wings booming, five birds touched down in the sandy bottom of the cut. "Remember the reward if we take them back alive," rasped the officer. He led, walking bent-legged and wary, twitching his sword before him like a feeler as if testing the air.

Mindful that four Guardsmen were still aloft, Fost didn't advance to meet him. Weapons ready, he and Moriana waited in the makeshift shelter.

The Guardsmen walked noisily through the brush. They walked around the ravine, swords swinging—and kept on walking. Fost stared at the soldiers' backs and looked at Moriana. She shrugged in surprise.

"There she goes!" a Guardsman yelled. He pointed his sword into the distance and his comrades lunged forward into the darkness that now shrouded the cut. Fost heard a clash of blades, then cursing. "She's gone again, dammit."

"Listen!" another voice shouted. "Over there! I hear them over there!"

A crashing through the underbrush told them the soldiers were blindly in pursuit of something that wasn't there. Now that skyriders could no longer see them, Moriana grabbed Fost's hand, and they ran in the opposite direction.

"I thought you said your enchantments wouldn't work against them," Fost said reproachfully as he gained the top of the rise.

"I did," said Moriana, "and they won't." Taking Fost's hand, she struck out across the fractured lands.

Later they lay side by side, huddled in blankets. With their pursuers afraid to venture after them, Fost had returned to his sled to gather what supplies he could. The dogs were all dead, killed by Guardsmen's arrows. Wigma had still been breathing, though barely. He had raised his head at the humans' approach. The reproach in his eyes was all for himself: *I tried, Master, but I could not fight them all.* He licked Fost's hand as the courier threw himself down at his side. His tongue left a bloody track.

The big dog laid his head in Fost's lap and died. The courier groped for words of farewell, but there was a catch in his throat and he wasn't able to speak.

Moriana had led the way through the broken country until she judged they were far enough away from their pursuers. She had hunted these lands as a girl, running down dire-weasels and fleet-footed antelope on Ayoka's sturdy back. She had found a place where the earth of a ravine's bank had fallen away, leaving a flat slab of shale to roof a shallow cave. They made their cold camp here, sharing gruel and lukewarm water.

"If you didn't cast some kind of spell of invisibility over us, who did?" asked Fost, stretching a finger to trace the line of Moriana's jaw.

"I don't know."

"If either of you had the sense the Three and Twenty Wise Ones gave a dung beetle, you might infer the identity of your savior." The peevish voice emerged from the satchel propped against the bank. "Though why I should expect gratitude from the likes of you I'll never know."

Fost drew himself up on one elbow, peering through the darkness at the spirit's jug. "You? But how?"

"Moriana didn't. *You* certainly did not. Whom does that leave?"

"I didn't know you were a magician, spirit. What else have you concealed from us? Remember the Josselits, Erimenes."

"No magic was involved. A mere trifle of mind control. Why, even when alive I could have accomplished such a feat with ease. My thirteen hundred ninety-nine years of contemplation have only honed the edge of my abilities."

Moriana's eyes met Fost's in the darkness. "The savants of Athalau were noted for their mental abilities, apart from sorcery," she said.

"Which explains how," the courier said, "but not why. Why, when you were on the verge of seeing our blood shed as you've so avidly desired before, did you rescue us?"

"Even if I felt called upon to account for my actions to some lout of a courier . . ."

"The Josselits, Erimenes. Remember them."

". . . I strongly doubt you have the mental capacity to follow my reasoning," the spirit said testily. "As for your incessant caviling about the Josselits, I can only observe that they would be as stimulating company as you've proven this night. Lying beside you is a lovely wench who owes her life and soul to you, and yet you lie there like a pious divinity student without doing a thing about it."

Erimenes's comment made Fost aware of an urgent tickle below his belt. He gazed at Moriana for a minute. Her expression was unreadable in the starlight.

"No," he said at last. "I think not. After what you've been through today . . ."

Moriana kissed him lightly on the lips. "Thank you, Fost." With that she rolled over, snuggled herself against him, and went promptly to sleep.

In a short time he too slept, but his dreams teemed with enemies and screaming faces.

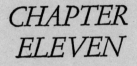

CHAPTER
ELEVEN

Like damp, rumpled cloth gradually dried and drawn taut over a frame, the land flattened from undulating prairie to a virtually featureless steppe. High gray-green grass, bowing before the ceaseless wind, stretched as far as the eye could see in all directions. Winter and the nearness of the polar zone had dropped a blanket of dreariness on the land. Leaden gray clouds rolled across the sky, building an impenetrable wall above the low, black bulk of the Rampart Mountains. Even the sunlight was robbed of its brilliance and cast a wan radiance. And every step took the fugitives deeper into bone-chilling cold.

Fost and Moriana had spent three days winding through the labyrinth of ravines. Twice flights of war-birds had flown over, but overhanging banks had provided them cover from observation. By the time they emerged from the broken country, not an eagle could be seen through the whole vast dome of the sky.

From there on, they had to traverse open country, which gave no shelter from the keen eyes of Rann's eagles. So they decided to travel mostly at night, halting at the first pallid tint of dawn to dig places to sleep away the daytime. The roots of the steppe grass reached deep. They knew they could cut up great chunks of sod and then pull them back into place over them to provide camouflage.

For their own reasons, the two felt increasingly eager to reach the city in the glacier and the treasure it concealed. Yet their path did not lead directly toward the Gate of the Mountains, the pass that lay due north of Athalau. The swallowed city rested on a southeastward line running through Thailot to Brev. The travelers' weary legs, however, carried them almost directly south.

Moriana broached the subject the evening they emerged from the ravines. They had just finished the celebration denied them the night of their escape from the City in the Sky. Facing one another, naked, they pressed close with the aftermath of passion.

"If we make straight for the Gate of the Mountains, Rann's men will have us before we go thirty miles," she said, the words slightly distorted as she lay with her cheek against the courier's chest. "Their eagles have poor night vision, but on the steppe they don't need to see well to make out moving figures."

"What can we do about it?" Fost asked as he absently stroked her golden hair.

"I remember hearing of a way through the Ramparts near the Great Crater Lake directly south of here." She rubbed her smooth cheek across his chest. "Synalon has some scheme in mind; I don't think she'll let Rann have many men to hunt us. He'll concentrate on the straight path to the Gate. If we make for the Crater Lake we'll have a better chance of eluding him."

"Hmmm," Fost rumbled thoughtfully to himself. "I remember something about a western passage on that map I took from Kest-i-Mond. I don't recall exactly, but I have the impression there was something ominous about the name."

"The Valley of Crushed Bones, it's called." Erimenes's tones seemed even more sour than usual. "If that sounds at all ominous to you."

"It does. But no name, however awful it sounds, scares me as much as Rann and his bird riders."

"Nonsense. You've dealt with the Sky Guardsmen before." Erimenes made a sound as though clicking a vaporous tongue. "Really, Fost, I cannot fathom your timorousness."

Fost made a rude noise.

"What became of the map?" Moriana asked him.

He grimaced. "Obviously Synalon knew its value. I had it in the satchel you stole from me." He felt her tense at the words and patted her rump affectionately. "Never mind. That's long gone by now. At any rate, I don't have the map any longer."

"And Rann does," Erimenes said. "He'll know of the westward route. He'll lay a trap for you, mark my words."

Moriana eased her head around to look at the satchel. "I have the feeling there's something about the Crater Lake country that our distinguished colleague dislikes. Why don't you want us going to the Great Crater, Erimenes?"

Erimenes mumbled something about them regretting such ill-considered judgments and spoke no more.

"Another mystery," Moriana said to Fost. "First he renders us invisible to the Guardsmen despite their protection spells. Now he displays this curious reluctance about the Great Crater Lake. I wonder what it means?"

"Nothing but good, if it shuts him up like that," Fost replied. He reluctantly pulled away from Moriana's grip and sat up, the cold wind from the steppes whipping around him. But the wind felt good, clean, fresh, and crisp after the blood and death they'd been through. "Let's be on our way. The night soon will be dark enough to cloak our movement from Rann."

"I suppose you're right," sighed Moriana. She straightened and stared southward.

Fost didn't have to be a mindreader to know what

she was thinking. On this score, their thoughts were as one. The City in the Glacier. The Amulet of Living Flame. Immortality.

Immortality!

They had endured much at the hands of Synalon and Rann. They had defeated them. Now only reward lay ahead for the courier and his princess in the south-lands.

"Come on, let's *move!*" Fost cried, struggling into his clothing. "The sooner we're off these steppes the better I'll like it."

"Yes, Fost," agreed Moriana, dressing as quickly as the courier. Neither could hide the soaring anticipation they felt.

"Why you're so eager to freeze, going in this direction, I'll never know," sniffed Erimenes. "There's nothing this way you could possibly want, mark my words."

But Fost and Moriana ignored him. They strode off onto the night-shrouded steppe with a spring in their walk, hand in hand, knowing the worst lay behind them.

Fantasy from Ace fanciful and fantastic!